"I thought I saw someone slip between the stores back there."

Aaron frowned. "I'd like to say we don't need to worry about it, but after all that's happened, I'm not taking any chances. Come on, let's get off the main drag."

He led them down the next street, taking a shortcut around the block before meeting back up with the main street again. The moment they walked up to the corner, Cally gasped. The shadowy shape was back, and it appeared to be a person leaning against a wall under a store awning. It looked as though the person was waiting for something—some*one*.

"Aaron..." Cally could_____ ice from wavering.

"I see him," Aaro_____ "Come on, we're almost to the statio_____

But as they took the fir_____ eir journey, Cally couldn't res_____ ver her shoulder.

She almost screamed.

The white-clad figure had started moving, and the person was running straight for them.

Michelle Karl is an unabashed bibliophile and a romantic suspense author. She lives in Canada with her husband and an assortment of critters, including a codependent cat and an opinionated parrot. When she's not reading and consuming copious amounts of coffee, she writes the stories she'd like to find in her "to be read" pile. She also loves animals, world music and eating the last piece of cheesecake.

Books by Michelle Karl

Love Inspired Suspense

Mountie Brotherhood

Wilderness Pursuit
Accidental Eyewitness
Christmas Under Fire

Fatal Freeze
Unknown Enemy
Outside the Law
Silent Night Threat

CHRISTMAS UNDER FIRE

MICHELLE KARL

⟠ HARLEQUIN® LOVE INSPIRED® SUSPENSE

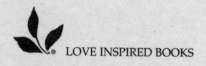

LOVE INSPIRED BOOKS

Recycling programs for this product may not exist in your area.

ISBN-13: 978-1-335-49075-9

Christmas Under Fire

www.Harlequin.com

Printed in U.S.A.

Come unto me, all ye that labour and are heavy laden, and I will give you rest.

—Matthew 11:28

To everyone who demonstrated patience and grace while I was writing this book.

You know who you are. Thank you.

ONE

Cally Roslin stepped out of the small airplane and shivered as a blast of icy northern wind cut through the dampness in the air. It seemed to slice into her heavy winter coat and snow pants and cling to her skin like a layer of frost. She'd experienced a Canadian winter before, but the late December temperatures in Toronto had felt nothing like this introduction to the climate of northern British Columbia. It made her miss the dry warmth of her homeland, the Kingdom of Amar. She clutched the edges of her puffy jacket's hood around her face to keep her cheeks from taking the full brunt of the cold and gripped the railing with her other hand. The thick glove she wore squished against the metal, and she had to squint to keep her eyes open as she descended the metal staircase to the tarmac.

She sighed in relief as she reached the bottom step. An attendant wearing an airport ID badge quickly ushered her inside the main building—which was the *only* building for passengers, as far as she could see. Cally had checked out the website for the Rocky North Regional Airport before boarding the tiny aircraft in Vancouver for the second leg of her journey, and so she'd expected the rural, unsecured facility to be small and sparse. But she hadn't realized *how* sparse until seeing it with her own eyes.

The terminal consisted of one open concourse with a few benches, vending machines, workstations and two side rooms marked as Gate One and Gate Two. The waiting areas for these looked about as large and exciting as her dentist's office—which was to say, not at all. She saw no other passengers and only one other attendant working behind a service desk. At least the place was clean and warm, with bright lighting to counterbalance the diminishing daylight outside and a selection of garish Christmas decorations to celebrate the season. Despite only being around four o'clock in the afternoon, the sun looked ready to call it quits for the day.

Cold, dark and a little lonely. It's what I wanted, isn't it?

Cally scanned the room a second time. In an email exchange, her local friend, Ellen, whose wedding Cally had used as an excuse to get away from her life in Amar for a little while, had mentioned that a Royal Canadian Mounted Police officer would be arriving to chauffeur her to a rental cabin in Fort Mason. The cozy place was to be her home for the next two weeks or so until the wedding, and she was looking forward to spending Christmas with her friend *and* finally having some blessed respite from everyone and everything else back home.

Cally had also received official communications from the RCMP before leaving for Canada, but was trying not to think much of it. The message had called her a foreign dignitary and said she'd been assigned a personal concierge for the duration of her trip, a federal law enforcement officer who she assumed was the same person Ellen had mentioned would be playing chauffeur.

But standing in the nearly empty terminal, Cally felt a twinge of relief at the absence of anyone waiting for her. She was no dignitary, and certainly not deserving of any special attention. Yes, she technically belonged to Amar's royal bloodline, but her claim to the throne was so distant that it barely counted. Back home, it afforded her the lowest possible level of privilege, in the sense of a title and special designation on official forms and documents like her passport—and it got her into certain special events on the guest list—but she lived an average, everyday life. Especially after the sudden death of her husband eighteen months ago in a tragic car accident.

These days, she spent most of her time taking on freelance graphic design projects and binge-watching home renovation shows, in an attempt to hide inside her small apartment and avoid unwanted advice and "help" from her overbearing family. Not that the strategy worked most of the time. They'd never approved of her marrying Esai, a non-Amaran she'd met as a university student, in the first place. She couldn't recall the last time she'd gone a full night without her mother or another relative phoning to tell her what she should do now that she was "free" and "back on the market." She'd tried to explain how much their words hurt, but they either ignored her pleas or refused to understand. Some days she almost missed the rigid schedule and isolation of Amar's compulsory year of military service.

"Excuse me, miss?"

Cally turned around to see the smiling female airport attendant taking tentative steps her way. "Yes?"

The woman clasped her hands together. "I'm so sorry, but the airport closes at four o'clock today, in five minutes. I see that your luggage has been brought inside, but do you have someone coming to pick you up? Or do you need help to arrange transportation?"

It closed at four? That wasn't something she'd accounted for—evidently she'd missed that on the airport website. But shouldn't her supposed escort have already arrived, in that case? "I...someone is apparently on their way. I'm sure he'll be here soon."

As the woman walked away, it dawned on Cally that she should probably freshen up before the drive to Fort Mason. The journey from Amar to northern BC had taken all day, and her teeth felt fuzzy. Five minutes was plenty of time to get the job done.

Cally rolled her suitcase from the back doors to a small alcove by the front entrance, then slipped into the ladies' washroom and headed for the wheelchair stall to hang up her winter gear before landing at the sink. She brushed her teeth, ran a brush through her knotted hair and swiped a coat of gloss on her dry lips. Feeling cleaner and more put-together than she had in hours, she ducked back into the washroom stall to bundle up again. A few minutes later, she was re-dressed and ready to go.

She stepped out of the washroom into a darkened airport.

"Hello? Anyone here?" Her stomach squeezed with confusion. Had everyone left and closed up for the day? How had they forgotten about her when her luggage was still out in the open—

She groaned. Because it wasn't in the open. She'd moved it off into the alcove where it wouldn't be in anyone's way. She'd done too good a job at being unobtrusive. The attendant she'd spoken to probably saw the empty space where her suitcase had been and assumed she'd left. Cally hadn't heard anyone come into the washroom, either, but then again, she'd left the stall door open while taking off her winter gear and putting it back on—so if anyone had glanced quickly inside, they'd have seen a full row of open stalls and surmised the room was empty.

The world outside the bay windows was dark, the sun's rays having almost fully disappeared below the horizon. She checked the front doors and discovered she wasn't locked in. The doors swung open when she pressed on the crash bar, but the world outside was nothing but parking lot and empty green space surrounded by heavy forest. If she left the building, the doors might very well lock behind her, and then she'd be out in the cold with no shelter. But what if her ride was still on his way? If he drove into the parking lot and saw a darkened building, he might simply turn around and leave.

Cally looked around for something to brace the door open a crack, to indicate somebody was still inside. Using her cell phone flashlight, she illuminated the space near the doors and saw a triangular doorstop. She shoved it under one of the doors, cracking it open by about ten centimeters.

Her stomach growled as she turned off her cell phone's flashlight to conserve battery. She took note of the reception icon, which indicated that she didn't have any service. She supposed that shouldn't come as a surprise, considering her remote location. There had to be a courtesy phone around that she could use to call a taxi or emergency services to let somebody know she'd been left behind.

She glanced across the terminal concourse, searching for a phone in the dim light. A vending machine gave off a faint glow from the inside, illuminating the potato chips and chocolate bars within—but more important, the soft light reached far enough to reveal a wall-mounted phone next to it.

Perfect. I can call for a ride and grab a snack for the drive, something to tide me over until dinner. She took a step toward the phone.

The shadows to her right shifted.

She gasped and flinched, but sensed no further movement. Had she imagined it? She swung her gaze from one side to the other, but the room's interior remained still and motionless.

And then the back of her neck felt prickly, as if she was being watched. She whirled around, but saw only darkness and the faint red glow of the emergency exit.

Maybe my original ride is finally here, she thought. *Maybe he's looking through the window wondering where I am. He could be in the parking lot right now, so I should probably check to make sure he doesn't miss seeing the propped-open door and leave.*

She took a step toward the front entrance, but glanced back at the phone and vending machine as a strange sense of wrongness washed over her.

Another shadow moved. Her insides twisted.

"Hello?" She whirled around, backing up to the entrance. "Who's there? I have a law enforcement escort and a killer left hook, so you'd better not—"

A rough swath of fabric plunged over her head, covering her face and blocking the dim light. She screamed as she felt a tug at her arms.

Someone is trying to kidnap me!

"Leave me alone!" she screamed and lashed out with her fists. The attacker grabbed hold of her wrists, apparently trying to control her flailing limbs, so she drove her knee upward instead—but her opposite foot slipped on the slick tile floor and her kneecap smacked into a bench. Her leg buckled beneath her, and her wrists were wrenched from her captor's grasp as she fell through the air.

Then she heard a bang. Something hard slammed into the back of her head, and the world went silent.

RCMP officer Aaron Thrace lunged through the airport's main entrance and caught the woman as she fell, centimeters before she landed on the hard tile. Had something or someone hit her as he'd rushed inside? A shadowy figure took off across the moonlit terminal and, before Aaron could even draw his weapon, slammed into the crash bar of a door underneath an exit sign on the other side of the concourse and plunged into the frigid night air. Aaron wanted to follow after the perp and serve immediate justice for whatever had transpired in the seconds before his arrival, but the safety of the person in front of him came first.

The woman groaned as she came to, her eyes hazy and unfocused. He sat her down on one of the plastic chairs by the door, keeping watch on both her and their dark surroundings. Why on earth had she been inside the shuttered airport all alone? He'd called ahead and told the attendant at the front desk that he would

be several minutes behind schedule due to traffic on
the highway from Fort Mason, and the attendant had
agreed to stick around until he arrived. Had someone
duped the attendant into leaving? He had to assume
that the woman in front of him was Ms. Roslin, the
dignitary from Amar whom he'd been assigned to escort and assist for the duration of her visit. What had
happened here?

"Ms. Roslin?" He pulled the swath of fabric, which
had been knocked askew, from her face, and her eyes
suddenly opened wide. She inhaled sharply and leaped
up from the chair, backing away with a fierce growl. He
held his hands up in a show of nonaggression. "Aaron
Thrace, RCMP. I'm not going to harm you, but someone just tried to. Are you injured?"

The snarl slipped away as her features relaxed. "Oh.
Oh! I don't…no, I don't think so. I was accidentally
left behind in the airport and then someone came out
of nowhere—"

Her gentle, lilting accent endeared her to him immediately, but intellectually he knew that was simply a
cognitive reaction to hearing certain types of accents.
Still, it was heartbreaking to hear a lovely voice like
hers recounting such an agonizing ordeal. "If you're
uninjured, will you be all right waiting here while I
search the perimeter?" She nodded but didn't look confident about it. "Are you sure? I won't be a minute. I'm
going to check outside of these doors and then confirm
it's safe to bring you to the car. Did you notice if your
attacker had a weapon?"

She shook her head this time, with greater resolution. "I didn't see one, but it was dark. The person
grabbed me with both hands. It felt like they were try-

ing to get me under control—like they were going to pick me up and take me somewhere? I'm not sure, sorry. They did shove something over my head first... oh, maybe it was that scarf on the floor?"

Welcome to Canada, he thought bitterly. "All right. Sit tight and don't move. Shout if you need me and I'll be back in a snap." He waited until she'd sat down again, then crossed the darkened concourse's perimeter. Whoever had attacked her might have simply taken off when their abduction attempt had been thwarted, but the Rocky North Regional Airport wasn't exactly located in a densely populated area. If anyone had driven off in a vehicle or run across the property to escape, Aaron was likely to spot the retreat. He hadn't noticed any other cars in the parking lot, though, which meant that her attacker was probably still lurking around a corner, waiting for him and Ms. Roslin to leave first.

Aaron rested his hand on his Taser but didn't draw it. Canadian regulations required him to keep his weapons holstered the majority of the time, until he had a perfectly good reason to draw one. And without a blatant threat in front of him, he simply had to pay close attention to his surroundings and be quick on the draw if necessary.

He leaned against the edge of the window and squinted into the darkness. If he'd known the scene would be so dark, he'd have brought night vision goggles. He thought he might have a pair in the back of his patrol car, but that was on the other side of the terminal concourse. He was unwilling to take his charge outside until he was certain she'd be safe—because even if the culprit had used both hands to grab at Ms. Roslin, it didn't guarantee that the person wasn't armed.

When he didn't spot any movement outside the windows, he glanced back at the woman. Her slight form was curled into the chair, knees pulled up to her chest and arms wrapped around her shins. She'd bowed her head, and he wondered if she might be praying. His heart tightened at her vulnerability, and he felt a sudden, unwanted tug at his core. To have come so far from home during what should be a joyful time of year, only to be attacked the moment she landed at her destination…well, that was a terrible way to start off a Christmas holiday.

His briefing on Ms. Roslin's visit had also mentioned that she was a recent widow, which he suspected might explain why she'd closed herself off so quickly. She was likely feeling frightened and alone. While he could never claim to understand what she'd gone through, the sense of loneliness resonated with him. His youngest brother, Sam, had gotten married earlier in the year, and his other brother Leo's wedding was scheduled for just a few weeks from now as a Christmas-themed affair. Aaron didn't even have a date to accompany him to the wedding.

Not that it bothered him. *Much.* He had a job to do, and that responsibility came first.

He checked the washrooms, turning on as many lights as possible as he moved from space to space. Both of the two small lounges designated as flight gates had their doors locked from the inside, so the attacker couldn't get back into the airport unless he happened to have a key to the main entrance.

Aaron jogged back to the front doors and gently

pushed the right door open. His patrol car sat about ten meters away—not too far, but hopefully at enough of a distance that he'd see anyone running at them with enough time to react. With no movement on either side of the building, and dim outdoor lights illuminating the front walkway under the entrance overhang, he made a decision.

"Ms. Roslin, I'd like to get you situated inside my patrol car. Are you ready to move?"

"Yes, please." She glanced around as though looking for something. "And I realize this might seem like a silly concern, all things considered, but what about my luggage? I don't mind if someone can bring it along later, but I might need to stop at a store for some basics on the way if that's all right. And if you think it's safe to do so."

"Where is it? Does it contain anything critical?"

She pointed to a dark alcove on the other side of the doorway. "It's standard size, rolling wheels. I have my passport and papers in my purse, but the suitcase has a bottle of melatonin tablets to help me sleep."

Not too critical, then. He suspected she'd be able to find melatonin at the pharmacy, so that wasn't a problem. It'd be an extra layer of complication and a potential risk to bring her suitcase along. However, the airport wouldn't open again until ten o'clock the next morning, and the backup he'd be calling to check out the crime scene would be coming from Fort St. Jacob, a slightly larger town located a few hours south of Fort Mason. Fort St. Jacob had more RCMP officers in their detachment, and unlike at Fort Mason, half of them hadn't temporarily left the area for the holidays—but it'd still be a significant burden on their already lim-

ited time for one of the Fort St. Jacob officers to bring
the suitcase up to Fort Mason.

He made a decision, found her suitcase and rolled
it over. It wasn't light, but he'd be able to lift it quickly
into the patrol car's trunk. "I'm going to get you into
the car first. If I deem it safe after the fact, I'll load the
suitcase. Is that acceptable?"

"Of course." Her eyebrows lifted in surprise. In retrospect, he'd been a little harsh with his tone, which
was unnecessary. She stood and unzipped the collar
of her puffy winter jacket, readjusting a chunky knit
scarf and a necklace that had somehow become tangled together in the scuffle, then zipped all her layers
back into place.

"Did you knit your scarf yourself?" He tried to put
her at ease, because he needed her to listen. When she
nodded, eyes wide at the strangeness of the question
in the moment, he knew she was paying attention. "It's
really nice. Okay, we're about to head outside. Wait for
my signal. Stay close. If anything happens, keep behind
me." He ushered her to the door, opened it a crack and
looked out a second time. *It'd be a great help if you
could give me an all clear, God.*

Instead, a light dusting of snow began to fall. As
peaceful as gently falling snow looked during the
daytime, right now it meant obscured vision in the
darkness—for himself and the attacker. It'd be annoy-
ing to drive through on the way back to town, but for
the moment, he'd have to try using the reduced visibility to his advantage. He unlocked the patrol car re-
motely, then scanned the area one more time.

"We go in three, two, one…and move." With his arm
draped over her back, he hurried her toward the car. He

surveyed the area as they moved, but they reached the vehicle without incident. He kept watch as she slipped inside. The coast seemed clear, which meant retrieving her suitcase was the right call. "I'm locking this while I get your luggage. I'll be gone only a few seconds."

He shut the car door before he could hear her response and jogged back to the terminal. He opened the airport door just far enough to slide inside, pull the suitcase out and close the doors. Because he didn't feel comfortable simply driving away with the front doors of the airport unsecured, he took a pair of handcuffs off his belt and clipped them around the handles. It was a pretty shoddy way to secure the place, but it wouldn't take long for additional RCMP officers to arrive once he called in the incident.

A rustling nearby made him pause. He squinted into the light around the front entrance. The falling snow—which had already grown denser—in front of the illuminated area made it hard to see into the dark spaces where the light didn't reach.

A sense of intuitive dread washed over him, and before his brain and body made the connection, a black shape darted out of the shadows…and headed straight toward him.

TWO

Cally muffled her scream with a gloved hand as the black-clad attacker darted out of the shadows toward Officer Thrace. She watched with helpless frustration as the officer withdrew his Taser and dropped into a firing stance, but the assailant changed course and sidestepped him, instead grabbing onto the handle of Cally's rolling suitcase.

What on earth...?

The aggressor must have underestimated the weight of the suitcase, because as soon as he—Cally could only assume the person was a he—wrapped his fingers around the handle, he lurched, momentum coming to a halt. Her breath grew shallow as Aaron jumped at him, looking prepared to wrestle him to the ground, but the man released the handle and bolted instead toward the patrol car.

Did the man have a weapon after all? She squished into the corner of the back seat, trying to make herself as small a target as possible—but right before the black-clad figure reached the car, he ducked and reappeared in the rear window, racing across the airport's property before plunging into the tree line of the forest that surrounded the facility.

Moments later, Cally grimaced at the heavy thud of her suitcase landing in the trunk. She pulled her gaze away from the trees and, out of habit, pressed her hand against the place her locket rested on her sternum. A gift from her uncle Zarek—the only relative who actually bothered to respect her boundaries and who hadn't treated her as a pariah for marrying Esai—the locket held a precious photo inside of herself and her late husband, one of the few her mother hadn't destroyed or deleted without permission after Esai's passing. She couldn't feel the locket through the numerous layers of heavy winter clothing, but knowing it was there brought her comfort. She closed her eyes for a moment to regather her bearings—and flinched as the patrol car door swung open with a creak.

"Not exactly the warm Canadian welcome you should have received," Officer Thrace said, slipping into the driver's seat. "Ms. Roslin, I'm so sorry that your first moments here were not positive. I assure you that the RCMP will be doing everything we can to figure out who that man is and what he wants, and the airport will undoubtedly be doing a thorough review of their closing procedures. Leaving you inside unattended was unacceptable, and you may be able to file charges, should you so desire."

She sighed, trying to release some of the tension in her shoulders. "I'm sure that won't be necessary, but I appreciate your concern. I'm just glad that we're all right. Are *you* okay?"

He twisted around in his seat to look at her. "I am. I have to call the incident in while we drive, but can you think of any reason why someone would go after you or your belongings? Does anyone know you're here who might wish you harm?"

That was the oddest and most incredulous notion so far. "No, I don't think so. Honestly, Officer, only a couple people know I'm here… I'm actually trying to get away from most of my family, if you can believe it." She chuckled without humor. "My friend Ellen knows I'm coming to visit, of course, but she's engaged to an RCMP officer, so I really don't think there'd be any connection that way."

"Ellen Biers, right? Her fiancé is my younger brother."

Well, *that* was news. "Really? Small world."

"Small town, more like. Look, if you can't see a connection, I'm going to go out on a limb and say it's likely that you weren't specifically targeted, but just in the wrong place at the wrong time. Considering you weren't noticed and got left behind inside the airport, it's entirely feasible that someone else could have hidden inside in order to commit a crime of opportunity. We've had some issues with theft and illegal weapons up north this year, so my gut reaction is that the individual was likely looking for something valuable to steal. He may have been trying to get a hold of you to snatch your purse or threaten you into handing over cash, valuables, the like. Trying to steal the suitcase seemed like a last-ditch effort from someone truly desperate—in need of money, trying to find something to steal and sell. Either way, like I said, it's unacceptable, and on behalf of the RCMP and the nation of Canada, I can't apologize enough."

If what had happened hadn't been so serious, she might have actually laughed in that moment. The man was so sincere and so concerned she almost hated to burst his bubble. "On behalf of, uh…myself, I accept your apology, and remind you that I'm nobody special. I don't need the nation of Canada's apology, nice as that is. I'm literally no one of importance, even in my own country—*especially* in my own country, so I'm honestly still a little baffled as to why I'm receiving a personal escort at all."

Not that she was complaining. She was very glad he'd arrived when he did, and he cut a heroic, imposing figure in the shadowy light. She had a feeling that once they had better lighting, she might feel the same way about the rest of his features.

And then she immediately felt guilty for thinking like that at all.

Esai had been gone all of eighteen months. That was it, and yet some days it seemed as though she'd been alone for as long as she could remember. The car accident that had taken his life had happened so suddenly and so unexpectedly that some days the lack of closure brought tears to her eyes without warning. Other days, she accepted the events as God's will. It was hard to balance the two, especially when the rest of her family continued to pelt her with their theories over what had happened in the accident, their opinions on Esai, and worst of all, their patronizing advice regarding Cally's love life now that she was "free" of him. In the past six months alone, she'd been the victim of no less than two "accidental" blind dates and three "good-natured" interventions. Why couldn't everyone just leave her be and accept that people processed grief in different ways and at their own pace?

When, and *if*, she was ready to love again, she'd know. And not a moment sooner.

Officer Thrace cleared his throat as he pulled the patrol car onto the road, and she tried to focus on the scenery outside the car window as he called in the incident. Thick flakes of soft snow fluttered past the glass and collected on the ground beside them as they drove.

He chuckled a few minutes later. "First time seeing snow?"

Heat rose to her cheeks. "No, but it's been a very, very long time. Why do you ask?"

"There's wonder in your eyes. That twinkle is almost as bright as the snowflakes outside. Just wait until the snow accumulates even higher over the next few days—you'll get the real northern Canadian experience. Might even get to see some snowmen in the yards if it's the right kind of fresh snow, or join in on a snowball fight at one of the community events coming up."

"There are different kinds of snow?"

He grinned, putting her at ease. "Just you wait. And for the record, it's not that it's necessarily about who you are that you're getting a personal escort, more about where you're from and where you've chosen to visit. Since you *do* have that Amar royal family connection on all your official documentation, plus this is a rather remote area and our countries have recently ratified a stronger trade agreement, the RCMP thought it would be wise to give you some, uh…"

His voice trailed off, but she had a feeling she knew what he'd been about to say. "Special treatment?"

"Well, yes."

"That's very kind. But not necessary." The window began to fog up next to her, and she rubbed it with her glove. "Though in retrospect, I do appreciate that you were scheduled to come to the airport. I'm scared to think what might have happened if you hadn't shown up."

He smiled at her through the rearview mirror. "I'd say that's God's timing, Ms. Roslin."

"Cally," she said. "Please just call me Cally. I'm here to get away from being Ms. Roslin for a little while, if you don't mind."

The conversation stalled as they drove, the snow falling thicker and faster on the dark road. Cally wondered how Officer Thrace could see anything as he navigated the route—the way the snow came at them, it looked like they were entering warp drive in a spaceship, like in one of those sci-fi movies Esai had loved so much. Her throat tightened at the thought.

"How far is it to Fort Mason?" she asked to distract herself.

"During the day and good weather, about thirty minutes. Right now, with the snow coming down the way it is…maybe another forty-five or so, hopefully less. RCMP patrol cars have high-quality snow tires on them. That sound you hear while we're driving? Those are the chains the detachment has put on around this time of year so we can make it through big storms and deep ice freezes without too much trouble."

Snow tires? Chains? Cally wondered what she'd gotten herself into. On the other hand, she'd wanted to get away from her old life. So what better way than to dive into a completely opposite climate, too?

The quiet in the car, save for the occasional chatter over the police radio, seemed to stretch thin. She didn't want to interrupt the man while he drove, but at the same time, she still felt jumpy from the attack at the airport and didn't want to dwell too deeply on those thoughts.

"Have you been in law enforcement for a long time, Officer Thrace?"

When he answered, she heard the smile in his voice. "If I'm to call you Cally, you might as well call me Aaron while we're in conversation. Fair?"

"Fair."

"And yes, I have. My father was in the RCMP and I followed his footsteps. I was part of the Musical Ride in Ottawa for a while—it's better if I show you what that is rather than explain it, but it's essentially a part ceremonial, part entertainment event where the participating Mounties dress up in our traditional reds and ride horses in formation. It's much more impressive than I'm making it sound, I assure you."

"It sounds lovely, and I'd be happy to learn more. I love horses, but I'm not much of a rider." She'd taken lessons as a child, but hadn't been on a horse more than once or twice since then. Before she could ask what kind of horses the RCMP used, the car slipped sideways with a sudden lurch. She gasped in alarm, but Aaron appeared to be unfazed. "Is this kind of weather normal?"

"Every winter," he said. "Some days—some *years*— it's worse than others, but the visibility isn't always this low. And these tires should help to keep us steady— they help grip the road if I need to correct quickly like that. The real danger is potentially not seeing other vehicles as they approach, especially when the space in the lanes is reduced and, like you can probably see outside your window, it's almost impossible to see the center line."

Potentially not seeing someone, like the man in the airport...who could be coming after me right now.

Cally tried to shove the thought away. It was irrational to think anyone was after her, especially after Officer Thrace—no, Aaron—had mentioned the area's issues with theft. Still, she couldn't help glancing out the rear window, searching for the glow of headlights or a shadowy movement on the road. How had the culprit gotten away? He'd run into the forest. Had there been a getaway car waiting? Surely he hadn't just hoofed it through the snow until reaching his destination.

"When the center lane is obscured, it can be a real challenge to stay positioned on the correct side of the road," Aaron continued, "though in rarer cases—"

She turned back around in her seat—and screamed as a massive black shape suddenly materialized in the road ahead of them.

Aaron shouted and swerved, yanking on the steering wheel so hard that the car slid and spun, the tail end careening sideways. When he tried to correct, the chains gripped hard and the car counterbalanced too far. The car pitched into the ditch, rolled forward and slammed into a tree with a jarring thump.

The airbag exploded with a bang. Cally's forehead banged into the seat in front of her, then smacked against the headrest as she was jolted backward. Pain shot through her head for the second time that day. Blackness tried to creep around the edge of her vision but she willed it away, adrenaline keeping her awake as she tried to make sense of the scene outside the car window.

She blinked away the sparks and moved her limbs carefully, touching her sides and the back of her head to check for injury. To her relief, nothing seemed broken or badly damaged. In the back of her mind, she knew that God had been looking out for them—but thanking God for keeping them from harm seemed like too much.

He hadn't been looking out for Esai, after all.

And then she realized that Aaron hadn't moved.

Aaron blinked, trying to stave off the pounding in his head as his airbag deflated. His immediate thought was for Cally, but he was having trouble forming the words. His mouth felt like it was full of cotton balls, and his teeth hurt.

"Aaron?"

Thank you, Lord. At least they were both alive.

He tried to move his arm and found that he could. He gave her a thumbs-up to indicate he was all right, but it occurred to him after the fact that she wasn't from North America and might not understand the gesture. Or it might mean something terribly rude in Amar.

"I'm all right," she said, preempting his question. "Though I have an awful headache. Shaken but otherwise unharmed. Do you need help?"

It took several more tries before he was able to force the words out. "Mildly battered and bruised, but the car took the worst of it. Not as bad as what might have happened if I hadn't swerved, though."

With the airbag fully deflated, he was able to twist around in his seat to check on her. Cally regarded him with a mixture of incredulity and disbelief.

"*You* swerved? We weren't attacked? I didn't think it was wise to swerve for anything in the road."

"Most of the time, no. It's not. But that was a moose, and you definitely swerve for a moose." He looked through the back window, trying to spot whether the animal was still on the road. If it was and anyone else came along during this weather, they might not have the benefit of snow tires with ice chains. Their swerve could have been much worse, especially if the tires hadn't slowed their momentum before they ran into the tree—or, in an older vehicle, he might not have been able to react in time to avoid hitting the massive animal.

Cally still looked confused, so he continued his explanation. "Surviving an impact with a moose is… unlikely. You hit a moose, and a disproportionate amount of the time, the moose is going to win. Fatalities are a strong possibility."

Color drained from Cally's cheeks. "In that case, I'm very glad that we're here in this ditch as an alternative. But how are we going to get out?"

He sighed and sat back in his seat, grabbing the radio handset as he did so. "We don't have a lot of resources in our tiny town during the good weather months, and during the winter it gets even more complicated. I'll call my brother to come pick you up in another patrol car so that you don't have to sit around and wait for the towing company. It'll get you to warmth faster, since it might take a little while for the tow truck to come."

She lowered her eyes, and guilt sliced through Aaron from head to toe. Some introduction to their country and their town he'd given her. Although neither the airport incident nor the moose in the road had been his fault, he couldn't help feeling he was already failing his first diplomatic mission—and truth be told, he suspected that this particular task had been given to him as a trial run. Among the members of his detachment, he had seniority. He'd been in Fort Mason for a long time compared to many RCMP assignments, a full eight years. His superiors had implied in several recent conversations that he was being considered for a higher position elsewhere in the country—perhaps back in Ottawa. And while he wasn't sure how he felt about relocating away from his brothers and his life in Fort Mason, the truth was that he'd started to feel a little, well…lonely, now that both Leo and Sam had wonderful women in their lives.

Not that Aaron would ever tell them that, though. He was the eldest Thrace brother, the responsible one. The brother unfazed by anything, who always kept his cool, who demanded perfection of himself and others.

And everything that had happened in the past two hours had been a far cry from perfect.

He radioed in their position so that Leo could come and pick them up, but it would be up to a half hour of waiting in the car. Without knowing the extent of the damage to the vehicle, he didn't feel comfortable running the engine while they waited—but that also meant they were about to get very cold, very quickly.

"Hang tight," he told Cally. "There's an emergency kit in the trunk with blankets, water and flares. I'm going to set the flares at the edge of the road to make our location visible, all right?"

She nodded and he climbed out of the car. Thankfully, the trunk latch hadn't been damaged in the crash, so it was easy to retrieve the emergency kit and set the flares by the road. By the time he returned to pass the blanket and water to Cally, her eyes were closed, head resting against the window. Her breathing had softened and her lips had parted slightly in relaxation.

Aaron draped the fabric across her, trying hard not to notice how lovely she looked as she rested. It pained his heart to think what might have happened to her if he hadn't arrived at the airport the moment he did. He hoped the officers from Fort St. Jacob who would be examining the crime scene would find something to lead them to the culprit. Trying to steal someone's belongings was one thing, but despite the reassurances he'd tried to offer up, he couldn't rule out the attack as an attempted abduction, either. Either way, he refused to let the act go unpunished.

I won't let anything happen to you, he thought. *Whatever it takes, I'll keep you safe.*

THREE

About an hour later, Cally climbed out of the second patrol car she'd ridden in that afternoon. In front of her was a cozy-looking cabin—more of a small house, really—which Ellen had promised would be "modern enough to have central heating, but rural enough to leave the doors unlocked at night." Cally imagined it'd look even better in daylight.

"Let me take a look around for you first," Aaron said, jogging past her and up the front steps. He opened the door—which was unlocked, as Ellen had predicted—and disappeared inside. Leo, Aaron's brother and fellow RCMP officer, grinned as he rounded the car to stand alongside her.

"If you need anything at any time, call him, okay? He's very good at his job, and he'll be upset if he hears you hesitated to ask." Leo scratched the back of his neck. "Plus, he's like…one of two officers on duty this week. I'm going down to Fort St. Jacob for my final tux fitting, and our youngest brother is teaching a training course with his wife in Vancouver until the end of the semester. They'll be back next week in time for the wedding."

"Congratulations," Cally said, and despite her own heartbreak, she meant it. "I wish we'd had our first meeting under better circumstances, but I have no doubt now that Ellen has found a good man who can keep up with her. But how is it that there are so few officers on duty? Doesn't the town need you?"

Leo shook his head. "Not particularly. We have a lot of seasonal residents during the spring and summer, so the population of Fort Mason and other small places up north tends to drop during the darkest and coldest winter months—December through February, usually—so the need isn't as great. Even then, few folks venture outside their homes. With only six hours of daylight right now and temperatures averaging negative twenty degrees Celsius for the next few months, the only time you'll see a lot of people at once is during the annual tree lighting ceremony in the middle of town on Saturday. We bring in extra officers, have a giant snowball fight, make maple taffy in the snow. There's a skating rink, too… It's great, you'll love it. People from all over the area come here to attend, sometimes driving hours just to see it. Ah, he's back."

Aaron sauntered down the steps toward them, house key in his outstretched hand. "All clear. Listen, I'm going to be at the station for the rest of the day, but is there anything we can get for you first? The fridge inside is stocked with some basics, but I'm happy to have food, supplies, toiletries or whatever you need brought over. We don't have a lot at this time of year, but we'll make it work."

"I'm sure I'll be fine. Do you normally leave houses unlocked around here?"

Aaron shrugged. "It's a small town. No one really locks their doors."

"But what about the thefts you mentioned?"

"Fort St. Jacob's problem, not Fort Mason's," Leo interrupted. "Not to brag about our small town being better than that one—"

"—which we grew up in—" Aaron raised an eyebrow at his brother.

"—but especially at this time of year, anyone comes into town who's a stranger, we'll know about it. Everyone here is your neighbor. We all have to band together and be there for each other in a place as far north as this during the winter. It's not unusual for folks to lend each other blankets or food or even a warm bed if a furnace conks out, for example. This town is full of good people."

"I'm glad to hear it." Cally looked sideways at Aaron as his brother walked away to return to the patrol car. "Thanks again for being there for me today. I'm still feeling a little rattled, but I'm sure it's nothing a good night's sleep can't take care of. Not that it's nighttime yet."

Aaron smiled. "Did I overhear Leo explaining how we only have six hours of daylight right now? It tricks the brain into thinking you're tired early and can be hard to get used to. On the other hand, there's a good possibility you might get to see the northern lights while you're visiting, especially if we get a night with clear skies. Anyway, like I said, you need anything, call. There's a list of emergency contacts by the landline inside, including the direct line to my personal cell. Call any time of the day or night."

He climbed into the patrol car with his brother and

waved as they pulled away. Cally waved back, feeling a pang of loneliness at being left by herself. She needed to get over that. She'd actually come up to the remote wilderness a few days early, before her scheduled girls' day with Ellen at a nearby spa—a place that Ellen insisted was the only reason tourists visited this part of the province during the winter months. She'd told herself she needed to gather her bearings and spend some time in quiet contemplation without a million voices in her ears.

But now that she had nothing but the silence she'd craved, the world seemed strange and empty.

And, despite herself, she really hadn't minded when Aaron was a part of it.

She willed herself to enter the house and explore the place she'd be living in for the next few weeks. Aaron hadn't been kidding when he'd said the fridge was stocked. She made herself a quick dinner, trying to enjoy the peace and quiet that she'd wanted so badly. But rather than sink into the moment, she felt uneasy—not relaxed at all.

With a sigh of frustration, she dumped her dishes in the sink and headed to the front door to search her purse for an aspirin. Maybe treating her headache would help her to settle into the place and feel less anxious about being alone after what had happened in the airport. However, her purse wasn't by the door. Nor was it with her suitcase, or hung up with her winter coat.

Did I leave it in the patrol car? She tried to visualize the ride to the cabin. She was quite sure she'd taken her purse with her when she'd switched patrol cars…but she couldn't remember grabbing it when she'd arrived.

And as much as she didn't want to burden Aaron after everything he'd already done for her, the plain fact was that her purse held her passport and travel documents, which she couldn't afford to lose.

She picked up the landline receiver to call him, trying to infuse her voice with an apologetic timbre when he answered. "Hi, Officer Thrace? It's Cally. I'm so sorry to bother you again, but I think I might have left my purse in the patrol car that brought me to the house. My passport and wallet are inside, so—"

"No need to apologize—I understand the importance," he said. "I'll go out and look for it. Hang tight. If it's out there, I'll bring it back to you right away."

She hung up and sank into the couch cushions, feeling grateful and a mite bewildered at his kindness.

I'm not quite ready to talk to You again, God, but... if this is Your doing, thank You.

Her eyelids began to flutter, exhaustion from the day beginning to creep in. It was still early evening, but she thought that once she had her purse back, she might grab a cozy mystery novel from the living room shelf and head to bed early.

Several minutes passed—or maybe more, it was hard to tell due to the perpetual darkness outside—before Cally heard footsteps heading up the driveway. *That was quick*, she thought, pleased and surprised.

She pushed up off the couch and headed to the front door as the doorknob began to turn. It was strange that Aaron hadn't knocked first, but maybe he didn't want to disturb her in case she'd fallen asleep again, like she had in the back of his car while they waited for the tow truck.

She hurried the final few meters to reach the door.

"Did you find it? That was—" But the words died in her throat as the edge of a white hoodie appeared through the crack of the open door.

Aaron hadn't been wearing a hoodie; he'd been dressed in his dark-colored RCMP uniform, and had told her he'd be on shift until late that night.

The person who'd opened the door wasn't Aaron.

She threw her weight forward, slamming her shoulder into the door. It caught the intruder off guard and sent him flying back with a shout. She didn't recognize the voice. The instant the door closed, she twisted the lock into place.

Then she bolted for the back door.

She heard what sounded like heavy footsteps approaching the back door from the outside, but she turned the lock first, then took off to find the windows.

She shivered, her body growing cold with a mixture of fear and anger, despite the heavy sweater and several layers of T-shirts she wore underneath it to stay warm. She checked all the window latches in the front hall, then proceeded to the kitchen, the bathroom and the bedroom. That left only one other area to check. She had no idea if the person was still outside, or if they'd taken off once they'd discovered the house was no longer an easy target—or a place to squat, which she supposed might also be the reason they'd come through the front door. But after the events of earlier that day at the airport, she refused to take any chances.

She crouched, moving toward the front living room with as much stealth as she could muster. Her heart beat a loud rhythm in her ears, making it difficult to listen for footfalls outside. Finally, she managed to find the courage to check each window lock. None of them appeared to have been compromised. She tried to take mental stock of the house—she'd checked all the other windows and exits. Hadn't she? She didn't know the rental property at all. It was entirely possible that in her haste to lock the front and back doors and the main windows, she'd—

A door creaked. It sounded as though it came from a far hallway, on the other side of the kitchen.

Yes, she thought, her entire body trembling. *I definitely missed one.*

Aaron climbed out of the unmarked patrol car he'd signed out for the evening and sauntered up the driveway toward Cally's cottage. He'd found her purse as soon as he'd opened the door of Leo's car. It had been wedged between the front seat and the center console, easily missed after all that had happened and in the excitement of finally reaching the cabin.

He tried hard not to imagine Cally's smile when he presented her purse—nor the way her entrancing brown eyes would light up with relief and happiness. It wasn't his place to think of her like that, or to think of her at all outside the boundaries of his obligations. She was his assignment, nothing else.

But still...

Movement flashed at the edge of his vision. He paused, listening. Was he seeing things? It might have been a skunk or a low-flying bat.

And then he heard a shout from inside the house, and he didn't waste another moment.

He bolted toward the noise, past the front door and around to the side patio. The patio door stood wide open, and sounds of a struggle came from inside.

Aaron plunged into the house, following the clamor. Only a few lights were on, but there was no missing the figure cloaked in white outside one of the bedroom doors. The ski-masked intruder was slamming his shoulder against the door in an effort to get inside, while Cally shouted at him from within the room.

Aaron dove at the man, tackling him at the waist. They fell against the hardwood floor, the impact jarring Aaron's knees and lower back. He tried to grab for the man's arms, intending to pin them back, but the angle at which they'd both fallen left the intruder's legs and feet too close to Aaron's face.

The goon slammed his heel into Aaron's jaw. Pain ratcheted through Aaron's entire head, momentarily blinding him. A second hit clipped the side of his forehead, and he felt the man slip from his grasp. He tried to regain focus as the assailant scrambled across the floor, shoved past him and Cally—who'd exited the bedroom and was trying to take a swing at the intruder with a side table lamp—and rushed back out into the cover of night.

Aaron rose, took two steps and stumbled.

"Aaron!" Cally bounded over and caught him by the shoulders before he toppled over. "Should I call an ambulance?"

"No, no." He tried to wave her off. The sparks in his vision were starting to clear, but he needed to call Leo right away and tell his brother which direction he planned to search for the home invader. "I need... I need to call..."

"You're not calling anyone. I'll do it."

Aaron pressed his back against the wall and slid to the floor. "Thirty seconds and I'll be on my feet again. That guy's kick packed a wallop. I wasn't expecting that."

Cally exhaled sharply. "I wasn't expecting someone to break into the house after all those promises everyone made to me about how safe this area is. I'd like to say there's a first time for everything, but I've had quite enough of that today, thank you."

How was everything going so wrong, so fast? He took several deep breaths, then pushed into the wall to stand again. His head still spun but he felt well enough to go out to the patrol car and call for backup. "Wait right here while I call this in. Lock the door when I step outside, and don't open it again until I knock. I'll go to the front door so you can look outside and see that I'm there."

He heard the click of the patio door's lock behind him as he left the house. It took only a few moments to call in the incident, and Aaron was still shaking his head in disbelief as Cally let him back indoors.

"I don't know what to say. Usually this area is incredibly safe. Our biggest issue for the past decade has been drug use and illegal weapons, save one incident earlier this year that had nothing to do with our town. It was an outside company's interference, and—you know what, it doesn't matter. What matters is that you're a guest in Fort Mason and we've done nothing but let you down at every turn, and you haven't even been here a full day. Are you all right? Did the intruder harm you in any way?"

His cheeks warmed at the look she gave him, a mixture of gratitude and skepticism. And here he thought he was too old to be embarrassed, but the events of the day so far made him, the town and by extension the entire province, look bad.

That potential transfer just keeps getting more and more unlikely... If she complained and the reasoning was found valid, he was certain there'd be an investigation into his ability to run the detachment, not to mention a possible demotion. It also didn't help that he felt a certain personal responsibility to ensure that she not only had a good stay, but an excellent one. It would make him happy to see her happy.

Because it was his job. *No other reason.*

She was attractive, yes, but she was also a perfect stranger.

Still, his heart hitched a little when a crooked half smile appeared on her face. Why was she looking at him like that?

"Your shoulder," she said, pointing to his arm. "You've got something hooked over your shoulder."

It took longer than it should have for her words to register, thanks to the hit to his head—*no other reason*, he continued to rationalize—but when he patted his shoulder, he remembered.

"Yes! That's why I was on my way over here so quickly." He pulled the strap of her purse over his head. "It was in my brother's car, between the front seats. Good thing I found it easily, or else I wouldn't have arrived as quickly as I did."

She took the purse and disappeared into the kitchen for a moment. Aaron checked and double-checked all the locks while he waited for her return. When she rejoined him, he couldn't help but note the weariness in her expression.

"Thank you," she said. "I guess it was silly of me to

think I could escape drama, regardless of where I go. I feel like it's following me. Not that being attacked in an airport and a home invasion are the same thing, but here we are and it's kind of feeling that way. Everything back home is so harried, everyone has things to say even when they should probably keep their mouths shut—" She paused with her mouth open, then flicked her gaze up to meet Aaron's with a look of mild horror. "I'm so sorry. I didn't mean to unload—"

"It's quite all right. I've checked all your locks and they're in good order. I wish I could explain why someone felt comfortable enough to waltz into this place unannounced, but I'm coming up short. My first thought was the person might be a squatter, but if that were the case, why not say something? And surely I'd have noticed some trash or disturbed blankets during my walk-through when we first arrived. I even checked the basement and didn't notice anything unusual.

"It's possible he was a standard home invader, but there aren't a lot of people in this town right now. We're going to notice anyone new, and if it was a local, well... my team should have this solved in due course. Rest assured that either myself or another officer will be going door-to-door first thing tomorrow morning and asking if residents have observed anything out of the norm or seen any newcomers lately. Leo is planning to delay his trip to Fort St. Jacob by a few days until it's dealt with."

She sighed and sank into the couch, resting her hands between her knees. "Thank you, but he doesn't need to do that. I appreciate the attentiveness, though. I keep trying to think of a reason why someone would want to harm me, but I simply can't imagine one. And like I said before, very few people know about my trip here."

Aaron pressed his lips together to think for a moment. "Would any of those people who *do* know be under the impression that they could get to the Amaran royal family through you? Either via abduction or otherwise?"

She laughed, but it was a bitter sound. "They'd have to be well versed in Amar's historical lineage, or have taken a close look at my passport. I mean, I suppose I'm in all the family tree information online, but someone would have to go looking for it. And to be quite honest, the connection is distant enough that I haven't spoken to those relatives for years." She paused, her voice growing soft as her gaze dropped to the floor. "Actually, that's not quite true. The whole extended family came to Esai's funeral, but it wasn't exactly the grand catching-up affair that would prompt someone to think there's enough of a relationship to matter. It was more a courtesy than anything. They're not bad people—please don't take it that way. The family is just very large, and that means the more distantly related, the more like strangers they are than family. Does that make sense?"

It did. "Apparently I have a whole host of third cousins living in Manitoba whom I've never met. And my mother's great-aunt has lived in south Florida for as long as I can remember, but I've never met her, either. So I understand. And I guess anyone who stopped to think about it logically would make that connection, too, but if I know one thing, it's that you can never assume logic when it comes to criminals."

Cally groaned and flopped back against the couch cushions, covering her face with her hands. "What am

I going to do? I'll be honest, I'm wary about staying here at all. What if that person comes back and tries to get inside again? What if he gets desperate and breaks a window? Or for all you know, he could be out terrorizing another family right now, looking for things to sell for drug money or guns or—"

"Hey." Aaron joined her on the couch and tapped her elbow. When she pulled her hands away from her face, several tears rolled down her cheek, leaving small streaks in her light pink blush. Her eyes, however, blazed with ferocity. "I have an officer out on patrol right now, keeping an eye on the town. Tonight, I'll be right outside your door. No one's getting into this house tonight, not even me." She began to protest, but he held up his hand to stop her. "I realize it's freezing out there, but we do have protocol for this type of thing. I have a portable, battery-operated heater in the car, someone is bringing coffee over and there's special gear I can wear to conserve heat. Tonight, you can sleep soundly knowing you're being watched over. What happens tomorrow, well, we should probably talk now about how that's going to go. What were your plans?"

She grabbed one of the pillows beside her and clutched it to her chest as she drew her knees up to sit cross-legged. "I was supposed to spend a few days here getting settled, and then Ellen was to come and take us up to the Rocky Mountain Spa for a pre-wedding pampering retreat. I was sort of hoping to put up a little Christmas tree in the house and try stringing lights like you do here. We have different traditions back home—we do streamers and use other types of plants for decorations—so I thought it would be nice to experience something new."

Aaron had experienced quite enough new things today, compared to the typically calm and quiet December of Fort Mason and the surrounding area. And as much as he wanted to give Cally the chance to take part in North American Christmas traditions right away, he felt uneasy about leaving her to her own devices, particularly after the home invasion.

"Here's an idea. Would you be willing to head up to the spa a few days early? I'll take care of the arrangements, and I'm sure Ellen wouldn't mind accommodating. I know she's busy with wedding prep, but maybe you can work on it together at the spa. It's a huge facility, really nice."

Cally's eyes brightened as she sniffled away the tears of moments ago. "You've been there?"

"I worked a few functions there, and have policed some community events. It's basically an all-inclusive winter resort." Not to mention he used to date the spa's owner, many years ago. Tricia had been a lovely woman, but they weren't right for each other. The breakup had been messy and difficult, and these days he often went out of his way to avoid policing spa functions or interacting with Tricia at all. The woman was a master at tracking him down, however. Maybe he could just drop Cally off without going inside.

Cally raised an eyebrow in surprise. "Then it's good for me and Ellen that she knows the owner, because I've seen the price we're paying and I'm quite certain it's far less than what a resort would charge. Yes, I'll go up early if it's in our best interest, for safety's sake."

He stood and adjusted his coat, mentally taking stock of the supplies in the patrol car he'd borrowed. He planned to double-check when he got outside, but as long as another officer brought him a thermos of piping hot coffee, he'd be all right until morning.

Cally gently brushed his sleeve before he could walk away. "Aaron, I do appreciate everything you've done for me so far, but if you get cold or tired, please come inside and use the couch. I'll give you the house key so that you can come and go if you want, all right?"

"That's quite thoughtful, but I won't need it."

She frowned and grabbed his hand, pushing the key into his palm. His skin felt warm and electric where she'd touched him, and he pulled away quickly. She blinked in surprise.

"Sorry," he said. "Tickles."

Her smile was gentle but sincere as she pointed at the door. "Go if you must, but if I find out in the morning that you needed to come inside and didn't, I'm going to be very cross. Don't even try to fool me."

He laughed gently at the sternness in her voice. "Okay, okay. I promise to take you up on your offer if it's needed. In the meantime, get some rest—I have a feeling you need it."

As he closed the door behind him, his smile slid from his face. He had no qualms about spending the night on watch outside the house—he was happy to do it, if it meant keeping someone safe. He'd do it for any of the townsfolk in a heartbeat.

What worried him more was the seemingly deliberate actions of the home invader.

The intruder hadn't been there to rob the house, or to retrieve items after squatting there while the place was unoccupied. No, the way he'd slammed his shoulder into the bedroom door had looked intentional. As if he was there to specifically harm Cally.

And combined with what had happened at the airport earlier that day, Aaron had a very bad feeling about the entire situation. The question to which he needed a fast answer, however, was whether he could find the attacker and take him down before he struck again.

FOUR

Cally had no idea how Aaron was still awake and able to safely drive after spending the entire night outside her rental cabin, watching over her. She'd had a difficult time falling asleep, despite trusting that he'd keep her from harm. Being in a new place for the first time was always a little disorienting, hence the melatonin in her suitcase, but worse were the flashbacks to the moment the man in the airport had dropped the covering over her head, thrusting her world into darkness and stripping her of control. She didn't want to think about it. It was bad enough that the car accident on the way into Fort Mason had surfaced old fears and grief about her late husband's death.

At least the RCMP officer assigned to her seemed kind, gentle and thoughtful. Aaron had understood her concerns right away and was going out of his way to help her recover some semblance of normalcy after yesterday. She had a feeling he was taking the attacks personally—the way he spoke into the police radio as they drove made her wonder if there was another reason behind the handsome officer's kindness, beyond the requirements of the job.

"This is the place," he said, slowing the car to turn down a long, snowy driveway. They'd woken up this morning to a world covered in massive swaths of fresh, white snow. It had taken Aaron an hour and a half to dig out the driveway so the patrol car could even make it onto the road, and by the time he'd finished, several new centimeters of snow had accumulated over his hard work.

This is normal for this time of year, he'd said. *Look at it this way—you're getting the quintessential Canadian experience!*

At the end of the long drive, an enormous, wood-exterior building came into view. It looked like a ski lodge, with giant windows, porches and a peaked roof. It evoked anticipation of a relaxing, luxurious experience, and Cally was ready for it. She'd never been to a place like this before. The most pampering she'd ever given herself, including before her own wedding to Esai, had been a manicure and a pedicure at the salon run by her cousin's best friend. She only got her hair cut once a year at most.

"This place looks far too fancy for me," Cally murmured, her sense of intimidation increasing as Aaron pulled up to the front doors. An attendant immediately bustled out to their car to take her bag and escort them inside, and once they were out of the cold and standing in the elegant interior, nerves flared in Cally's stomach. What on earth was she doing here? Why had she taken off from her family without telling them where she was going?

That wasn't entirely accurate—she'd left her mother a message explaining she'd decided to attend Ellen's wedding after all, and her mother had read the invitation. Still, Cally had received four emails and missed seven calls from various family members since arriving in Canada, but she'd answered only one, to let her mother know that she had arrived safely and that yes, she would return home eventually. While that might have been enough to pacify her father, her mother had grown even more protective since his passing several years prior. It didn't help that she was an only child, too.

She waited while Aaron spoke to an attendant, probably confirming whatever arrangements he'd made the day before. When he finished, he joined her where she waited, mild disappointment in his eyes—or was that annoyance?

"It shouldn't surprise me given the snowfall we had last night, but Ellen isn't going to make it up to Fort Mason today. The area south of us got hit even worse than we did, so they're still working on getting the roads plowed both inside and outside of town."

That *was* disappointing, but she'd already wondered if Ellen would make it, based on the size of the drifts she'd seen on their way to the spa. Some of the snow piles had been nearly as tall as her.

"Did she have an estimate of when she'd get here?"

Aaron shook his head. "Not specifically. It'll be when the local weather service and the RCMP give the all clear to get on the main highway. It's too cold to risk driving in conditions like this—sliding off the road could mean waiting for help in dangerously freezing weather for hours, depending on when help can come and how easy it is for them to find you. Leo found our car quickly last night because I had flares in the trunk, but not everyone has them in their emergency kit—despite how often we recommend it to the public."

Cally shrugged. "I can wait. I have this lovely spa to relax in, so I'm sure I'll find something to do. Are you heading back to the station?"

"Leo's going to relieve me so I can get a few hours of rest. If you need anything, however, don't hesitate to call. Like I said yesterday, I'm happy to assist in any way I can."

She thanked him again for his help and watched through the window as he returned to the patrol car and pulled back down the long driveway. And while she was relieved to be in a beautiful facility dedicated to ensuring her full relaxation, a most peculiar thing happened. As the car drove farther away, Cally's shoulders tightened.

And she began to wonder whether, without Aaron present, she'd be able to relax at all.

Once the spa building's exterior was no longer visible in his rearview mirror, Aaron stopped the car and got on the radio. With Cally securely ensconced for a few days of pampering with her friend, it was as though Aaron's body knew he didn't need to be on high alert anymore. His eyelids flickered, sleep threatening to finally overtake him. His mind fought against the tug of oblivion, however, because no matter how he'd tried to puzzle over the events of yesterday, it still didn't make complete sense.

He'd called the airport in the morning and followed up with the Fort St. Jacob RCMP who'd checked out the scene. Security camera footage was currently being combed through, but initial suspicions from the other town's team matched his own—that the individual had hidden inside the airport until closing, possibly seeing Cally go inside the washroom and not come out. It was also possible the individual had orchestrated some kind of distraction to ensure that the washroom wasn't checked, but either way, the employees working the terminal last night were in hot water for sure.

But Aaron doubted the individuals would get more than a slap on the wrist, unlike at a large, national airport. Rocky North Regional was an unsecured airport, meaning that it was too small to offer security screening of any kind. Anyone flying into Vancouver or another major center in the province was forced to go through security before entering the main terminal, just like any other passenger, but not here.

Things worked differently in the remote north, and Aaron understood that. He just hoped that Cally and the Amaran consulate did, as well, if she chose to report the incident.

He called his brother, hoping for an update. Leo picked up almost immediately.

"Hey," Leo said, "how are you holding up? The western road out of town is clear and the trucks are making good progress south, but apparently a bunch of folks tried to drive this morning, so there are at least three stranded vehicles between here and St. Jake's. Emerg is trying to reach them before the frost-bite does."

Aaron rested his head against the back of the seat and closed his eyes. "My body's about three seconds from knocking me out, but otherwise all right. Ms. Roslin is at the spa, waiting for Ellen, who probably won't make it up until tomorrow. I'm sure she'll find things to do, even if it's just napping in a peaceful room without worrying about home invaders. She's checked in for an overnight stay."

"Speaking of home invaders, there were no additional disturbances last night that we know of. I had Hatch canvass the area, but we've got nothing so far. No one has noticed any newcomers, which is even more bizarre. It's not like there are many places for folks to hole up without anyone seeing."

"Unless they're in someone's home. We've got plenty of empty houses, and if someone is careful, they could absolutely hide inside. And while I really hate to think that the airport attack and the home invasion are connected..."

Leo clicked his tongue. "Speculation, bro. It's an angle, but there's a decent distance between here and the airport. The suspect would have needed transportation between the two, and to know where Cally is staying. You didn't see any other vehicle and no one has noticed anything new, so we have to write up the report as if they're unconnected first. A connection is officially just a theory for now, until we have hard evidence. But I'm on your side here. Fort Mason is too quiet of a town to not consider the strong likelihood that these incidents are linked."

His brother made some excellent points. And if anyone knew a thing or two about connecting the dots between seemingly unrelated events, it was Leo. Leo had gone through a rough couple of days earlier in the year when the corrupt staff sergeant of the Fort St. Jacob detachment had targeted Leo's now-fiancée, Ellen, after she'd witnessed an accidental homicide. The way the law worked, until they had a direct link to tie the events together, they needed to be treated as separate, unconnected incidents.

"You're right. Hopefully there won't be another invasion, but if there is, we'll have to re-examine the evidence." Either way, he was having a bit of trouble with the concept of leaving Cally alone at the spa. He also hadn't seen Tricia when he'd checked Cally in, so it was possible she wasn't working today or hadn't made it in due to weather. "You think anyone would complain if I went back up to the spa and took a nap? I'm off the clock, and I'm honestly not sure it'll be safe to drive home. It means keeping the patrol car out here for longer than expected, though."

Leo chuckled. "You're the senior officer here, man. Do whatever you want. You have a change of clothes in the back of the car?"

"I do." He hung up and rubbed his eyes. The snow had continued to fall, much lighter than earlier this morning, but he still had a feeling that between the exhaustion and the blowing snow, he risked disorientation. Going back up to the spa seemed like the smart move, even if the only thing he could afford was a free bench in a stock room to lie down on for a few hours.

Plus, then he'd be close to Cally in case she needed him. Not that he thought she would, but just in case.

Just in case I *need* her, *is more like it*, came the unbidden thought, followed by a rush of guilt. The woman was clearly still grieving the death of her husband, and she'd come here to escape the anxieties of life. Plus, she lived in another country on the other side of the world. Moreover, she was an assignment. A possible stepping stone in his career.

Not a romantic prospect. That would be totally inappropriate.

And yet, despite the reasons his brain kept trying to throw at him, his heart still couldn't wait to see her again.

Cally was trying very hard to be present and in the moment, but she'd never been all that good at forced relaxation. The spa's interior was as gorgeous as the exterior, and the attendants had gone out of their way to show her around the facility and point out all the amenities and various services offered. Everyone was friendly and welcoming, and yet she was unable to shake the feeling that someone was looking over her shoulder, no matter where she went. Not that she'd gone much of anywhere since the airport, but she supposed being attacked twice in one day in a new place—not to mention the car accident—could make a person extra jumpy.

I should have asked Aaron to stick around.

She'd felt safe with him nearby, and while she had no doubt the spa had some measure of security, it was hard to have a lot of faith in how comprehensive it would be in an area where few people even bothered to lock their doors at night.

"Right over here, miss," said one of the female attendants, pointing to a cushy-looking chair with a steaming footbath at its base. "You look tense. Can I grab you a coffee or tea?"

"Tea, please." Cally slid into the seat, pulled off her shoes and socks and dipped her toes in the little bath. Ellen had recommended she get a few of the massage treatments to start, in an effort to relax and shake off the jitters caused by the day before. The warm water felt lovely on her feet, and the lavender-scented oils in the water's steam seemed to be starting to work their magic. At this rate, she'd be warm again and able to shed a few layers in no time. She tried to close her eyes for a moment…but a thump outside the door sent her adrenaline racing. She shivered, despite still wearing a sweater and long-sleeved T-shirt underneath.

"Hello?" she called, but received no response. Had she imagined the sound? She was probably just high-strung from the day before. It could mean anything, from a door closing to an attendant setting down a heavy vacuum cleaner.

Cally took a deep breath to chase away the flare of alarm. She left the chair to grab a white plush robe off a hanger by the door, then slipped it on over her sweater, the extra layer of warmth feeling both comfortable and protective.

She returned to the footbath, but it seemed to be taking an awful long time for the attendant to bring her refreshment. Using the call button by the door, she buzzed for assistance—but as she released the buzzer, the door swung open and a male attendant with a surgical mask over the lower half of his face and a scrub cap over his head stepped into the room.

Cally frowned, feeling awkward and a little alarmed about the attendant entering the room without knocking. "Hello? Who are you? The woman who was here a few minutes ago—"

"RMT," he said, his speech low and staccato.

Cally shook her head. "You're my Registered Massage Therapist? No, thank you. I'd prefer the other attendant to do the foot treatment, if you don't mind."

The intensity in the man's eyes made her suddenly very uncomfortable. "Actually, I'll just head to the washroom while I wait for her—"

She reached for the door, but the man slammed his palm on the wood, holding it shut.

"Sit down," he snapped. When she didn't move, he pulled a cell phone from his pocket and moved it toward her. She flinched back in alarm, clutching the edges of her robe.

"What are you doing? Please leave."

"Heart rate monitor before massage, standard safety procedure," he said, without missing a beat.

Cally had an incredibly weird feeling about all this. Where was the woman who'd come into the room with her first? "I don't think so. I've never heard of anything like that before. I'm leaving."

When he didn't remove his hand from the door, Cally knew something was very wrong. She swallowed down a rush of panic, then backed away toward the chair and the footbath.

"I really need to go," she said, pressing her back against the arm of the chair. A tray next to it held implements for her pedicure—clippers, cuticle oil and a nail file, among other things. She slipped one hand behind her back and wrapped her fingers around the nail file. It had been years since she'd completed her compulsory service in Amar's military, but she hadn't forgotten everything about self-defense.

The man began to advance on her, leaving the door unguarded.

Good, she thought, *just a little closer...*

"Please take a seat," the man said, and something

about his speech sounded strange. But with her pulse racing in her ears, she couldn't pinpoint what it was.

"I've already said no," she growled. Hadn't Aaron said this place was secure? "I've already asked you to leave and I won't ask again."

Even with only his eyes visible through the mask and cap, she saw his patience vanish, replaced by anger. His steps toward her quickened. Cally took a deep breath, steadying her nerve.

The instant the man was in arm's reach—his own hand extended as if to grab her—she whipped the nail file from behind her back and slammed it into his biceps.

He screamed in pain, stumbling backward, knocking over tables and trays. Cally didn't waste a second of the opening she'd created—she shouted and dove for the exit, banging her hand onto the call button at the same instant as she flung open the door. The hallway outside was empty.

She was almost free! Footsteps pounded from elsewhere in the building, coming closer.

She took a step forward and opened her mouth to scream for help again—and a hand clamped over her lips, muffling all hope.

FIVE

Aaron had just lain down on a futon in one of the empty massage therapy rooms when he heard a thump and a scream. *In the spa?*

He leaped up and raced toward the noise. The sounds of banging, like someone flailing around and knocking things over, raised his pulse and his speed. He passed a bewildered attendant hurrying down the hall, barely registering a sense of familiarity about the person, and turned the next corner to see Cally lurch backward as someone's hand closed around her mouth. She stood in a doorway, and her eyes widened at the sight of him.

Her entire body tensed and she dropped to the ground, escaping her captor's grasp. Aaron could see it was a man, slight with broad shoulders—possibly the same man Aaron had grappled with twice already.

And both of those times, Aaron had lost.

This time Aaron could see directly into his opponent's eyes, however, and it wasn't a good thing. The man clearly recognized Aaron from their previous encounters...and knew the odds based on yesterday's outcomes.

"His arm!" Cally shouted, rolling away from the attacker and swiftly rising to her feet. "He's injured, go for his arm!"

Aaron saw the man's confidence falter. *And there's my opening.*

Aaron lunged forward to close the gap and finish this, but instead of coming out to meet him head-on, the man backed up and slammed the door. A loud click told Aaron he had locked himself inside.

"Why would he do that?" Cally blurted.

"I don't—"

The crash of breaking glass sent Aaron back into motion. He hurled himself against the door shoulder-first, the wood splintering with each hit, until finally it buckled and he stumbled inside.

A blast of frigid air swept through the room as a figure launched off the windowsill, dropping from the second story to the ground below. Aaron rushed to the empty window and looked down, bracing himself for an ugly scene—instead, he saw an imprint of a human body, tiny red specks of blood and footprints that were rapidly disappearing under the heavy snowfall.

"Is he...?" Cally murmured.

"Nope. The snow cushioned his fall. It might have hurt a little, but with all the accumulation we've had lately..." He released a long breath through his nose. As frustrating as it was that Cally's attacker had slipped through his grasp again, the fact remained that Aaron had been here to stop him from harming Cally further.

Thank you, Lord. Guess there was a reason I stuck around after all.

He pointed to the floor where Cally stepped as she moved closer to the window, drawn by curiosity. "Be careful, there's glass all over the place and you've got flimsy slippers on. Are you hurt? Will you be all right if I run outside?"

She waved toward the door. "Go! Before he gets away for good!"

Aaron rushed after the intruder, passing the attendant who'd been on the way to the room, and slipped out the closest emergency exit.

When he reached the door, he ran outside and looked both ways, hoping for some sign of the direction the man had traveled, but the falling snow was so thick he could barely see more than a few meters ahead. His own footprints on the path were obscured almost immediately by the heavy snowfall.

Frustrated, he stormed back inside. Cally sat on the floor outside the room, her back against the wall and knees tucked up to her chin. She gripped the sides of her head, fingers twined through her hair, squeezing every few seconds like a pulse. After a moment, she sighed. "Please tell me you have an explanation for what just happened."

"I wish I did." He rested his hands on his hips, feeling the weight of the past day. "Are you sure you're all right? I feel like I'm asking you that nonstop."

Cally looked up, sliding her hands down the sides of her face. Her lipstick was smudged, making it look as though she'd cut her lip. "I'll be all right soon. Someone is getting me some water and an aspirin. My neck hurts from when that man pulled me backward. I'm so confused… I thought this place was supposed to be secure?"

"I thought so, too. I'm so sorry, I'd never have even imagined… Did the attacker say anything to you? How did he get into the room?"

She flinched. He hated to force the memory so quickly, but any information to help figure out what on earth had happened would be beneficial.

"He came inside implying he'd be doing my massage—the foot massage—and then pulled out a cell phone saying he wanted to use a heart rate monitor on me. He was super insistent that I sit down, which made sense at first because he claimed to be a massage therapist, but he was acting strangely."

"Heart rate monitor? Now I'm even more confused. Unless…" Aaron had a sinking feeling, but he wasn't sure if he should voice the concern out loud before giving the theory more thought.

Cally was having none of it, though. "Say it, please. Or…what do you say here, 'Spit it out'? I can see your brain spinning through your face."

He felt his shoulders rise as tension increased across his upper back. "Cally, I know you don't want to think any of these attacks are related to your family status, but you said he pulled out a cell phone? And he didn't harm you right away but tried to put you at ease, albeit rather poorly? To me, it sounds like the makings of another attempted abduction—like he wanted to preemptively take a proof of life photo in case the kidnapping got you banged up or worse."

Her brow creased as she frowned. "What are you talking about? Proof of life?"

He swallowed, trying to force the words out around the tightness in his throat. "Cally, I think whoever is after you wants to kidnap you for some reason or another. And based on the way their abduction attempts have been going…taking you alive and unharmed might not be a priority."

* * *

Cally felt like she might be sick, though she partially chalked that up to the pain along the sides of her neck. So it might be abduction after all? *Her?* It made no sense. It was impossible. She was a no one, an outcast by choice. If a kidnapper wanted ransom, she'd probably rot in their clutches before her family agreed to pay any kind of exorbitant sum—and besides, her family didn't have the kind of money kidnappers might ask for in the first place. Like she'd told Aaron, she barely knew or saw her actual higher-up relatives, and *they* were the ones with money and influence.

"Well, he's now failed three times in a row, so maybe these ridiculous attacks will stop. I'd be giving up and moving on to an easier target if I were him. What I can't figure is how someone knew that I'd be here. We didn't notice anyone following your car, right? For that matter, has it really been the same person all three times?"

Aaron massaged the side of his temple, grimacing. "I'm quite certain. I'd initially thought the airport attack was unrelated, but now I'm willing to admit they're tied together. How this guy knows where you're going to be, though…I have no idea."

Cally suddenly felt very tired. "So much for a relaxing spa day. I feel ready to go back to bed."

"I hear you. And while I'd love to tell you that we can stay here all day and rest, I need to get back to the station and help organize the investigation into what's happened so far. I'm not sure I'm comfortable with you remaining here on your own. Clearly the security isn't as tight as I'd assumed."

The blonde attendant who'd run off to get Cally

water and aspirin returned as Aaron spoke, agitation growing on her face with each word. "Excuse me, Officer, but we've never had anything like this happen before, I assure you."

Aaron flinched as the attendant came into his line of sight. "Tricia." He nodded at her in acknowledgment. "I didn't realize you were here today." The woman raised her chin, apparently indignant at his words.

"I could say the same to you." Tricia brought the water and aspirin to Cally, handing them off with an apologetic smile. "I'm so deeply sorry, Ms. Roslin. If there's anything else I can do—"

"You can start by upgrading your security system," Aaron cut in. "Should I assume the doors throughout the facility aren't locked during operating hours?"

Tricia raised an eyebrow. "It's never been a necessity. Sometimes clients like to step out for a breath of fresh air or some other reason, and the doors are open so they can come and go as they need to. We've never had an issue."

Aaron crossed his arms as Tricia took a step closer to him. The air seemed to fill with tension, and not in a good way.

"Sorry," Cally said, speaking slowly. "But am I missing something here?" She hoped her tone implied her meaning. When the two people across from her locked eyes, Aaron looked away from the woman first. Tricia didn't respond, either, but appeared to have greater trouble pulling her gaze from the Mountie.

"We have security tapes in some areas," Tricia said, directing the information at Cally. "I'll go see if I can pull the footage."

Tricia took off and Cally turned her attention back to Aaron. "So…?"

Aaron cleared his throat and looked anywhere but at Cally. "We used to date. It didn't end well."

Now their interactions made a *lot* more sense. "Let me guess—you ended it."

Aaron's eyebrows lifted. "How did you know?"

Cally couldn't hold back her smirk. "Call it a woman's intuition."

"Huh." Aaron stepped closer to lean against the wall beside her. "Cally, are you sure you're all right? This is a lot for anyone to handle, and I suspect even more challenging for you, being away from home and your support system."

She shrugged. "I'm not sure. In some ways, I feel like I've dealt with enough senseless tragedy in my life that I'm uniquely equipped to handle situations like this. And it's not as if I even have a strong support system at home anyway." A wave of sadness washed over her, and she tried to shove it aside. Denying her emotions didn't always work, though, and that was okay. She'd rather feel something than live a life of emotional repression. "Other times, I wonder if maybe God's trying to teach me a lesson and I'm not getting it. I want to shout, 'Okay, God, You've made Your point!' but clearly there's something I'm missing."

She paused as one of her deepest fears surged to the surface. Aaron didn't need to hear it; she didn't need to trouble him with the vocalization, but at the same time, a part of her wondered whether sharing it with someone else might make the burden lighter, validate the thoughts that roiled around inside of her.

She took a deep breath and continued. "Sometimes

I fear that He took Esai away from me to teach me that lesson. Maybe I was too defiant, or asked too many questions about my faith. I've always been a bit of a wanderer—spiritually, intellectually, academically—and not everyone in my life has appreciated that. Even now, after Esai…not much has changed. Here I am, thousands of miles from home at Christmas because I can't handle being around the people I'm supposed to love unconditionally. What if God is angry at me? What if He decides to teach me another lesson and takes away one of the other few people I trust?" She touched the front of her sweater, feeling the bump of her locket underneath all the layers. Heat rose behind her eyes, and she tried to blink it away as Aaron knelt next to her.

"I don't think that's how God works, Cally. In fact, I know it isn't. But I hear what you're saying. After I'm done with my reports and we're feeling a little less shaken by immediate events, let's come back to this conversation, okay?"

Cally couldn't help smiling. "Yes, sure. I'd like that. Thank you for not telling me I'm crazy to think that way."

"I'd never call someone crazy," he said, standing. "First, that's insensitive, and second, it'd be invalidating your feelings. Feelings aren't facts, so you have every right to feel the way you do. Need an assist?"

She reached for the hand he'd outstretched to help her to her feet. The moment she slid her palm against his, it felt as though an electric current traveled up her arm and down her spine. She met his eyes with a silent gasp, wondering if he'd felt it, too, and found him staring at her as if seeing her for the first time.

Several seconds passed, and neither of them let go. Cally wasn't sure she wanted to.

Aaron's lips parted, and he seemed to be closer to her than he'd been moments before.

What is happening? Cally's breath felt stuck, and a light buzzing rang in her ears. *And how come I'm not trying to stop it?*

His fingers tightened around hers, and that electric current zipped through her a second time.

"Aaron," she whispered. "I—"

"I've put all the afternoon's footage on—" A chipper voice rang out as footsteps clacked around the corner. Tricia reappeared and instantly froze. Her voice turned flat and cold. *"Oh.* I'm sorry, am I interrupting something?"

Aaron released Cally as if she were on fire and stepped toward Tricia with a detached expression. He took the USB stick Tricia offered and glanced over his shoulder, speaking to Cally while avoiding eye contact. "You coming? We should get back to the station before the snow makes the roads impassable again."

Then he took off, leaving Cally standing in the hallway with Tricia. She felt as if she'd been sideswiped.

Okay...what just happened?

And for a moment, she wasn't sure which event she had more questions about—the theoretical attempted abduction, the inexplicable pulse of attraction between herself and Aaron, or the fact that their shared moment had turned to ice the instant his ex-girlfriend reappeared.

Worse, she wasn't sure she even wanted all the answers.

SIX

An hour later, Aaron brushed the snow off the patrol car with perhaps more force than necessary. Despite the awful weather and fast accumulation on the roads, he'd recognized that he needed to take a quick nap before attempting the drive back to town. No use courting even more danger. He still felt exhausted, but not nearly as fuzzy as when he'd first dropped Cally off. He was confident in his ability to get them back to town now, and planned to rest more afterward.

The events of earlier replayed in his mind as Cally exited the spa and moved toward the car. What had he been thinking after the attack, getting swept up in Cally's moment of vulnerability? She'd looked so beautiful and trusting as she confided in him, and his heart had ached for her loss and for the thought that anything bad could ever happen to a woman like her.

He'd been caught by the adrenaline rush after being in a high-stakes situation with her, and of course that was going to cause them to psychologically depend on each other and possibly even build a false sense of attraction. Because that was what it had to be—false. Yes, he found her *physically* attractive—that dimple on her cheek threatened to undo him every time she smiled—but despite the seeming compatibility of their personalities so far, what did he even really know about her?

And beyond that, she wasn't even a Canadian citizen. She lived halfway across the world! And she was still grieving the loss of her husband. Nothing about his attraction to her was professionally appropriate or logistically feasible. True, she hadn't pulled away when their palms met, or when they'd seemed to be drawn together like rare-earth magnets, but it had to be a result of the excitement in the moment.

He'd be tossed out of consideration for promotion for sure if he got himself tangled up with the very dignitary he was supposed to be serving and protecting.

With the windows finally cleared of snow, Aaron climbed back into the patrol car and checked on his passenger.

"Ready to go? This could be a bit of a long drive, as we'll have to take it slow. The accumulation has been really fast since this morning, but hopefully by the time we get back onto the main road, the plows and salters will have come through."

Cally used her sleeve to wipe away condensation on the window. "When I decided to fly here for the wedding and for Christmas, I knew it would be cold and snowy in Canada. I guess I didn't realize just how unpredictable the weather would be."

"That's the thing about being up north and near the mountains. Things change quickly and often with little warning." He drove down the spa resort's driveway at a crawl. One of the attendants had gone outside with a ride-on snowblower to clear the way, and she waved as they passed by. Aaron waved back in gratitude. "And again, I apologize that your first and second impression of our province isn't exactly positive. Whoever is responsible for these attacks won't be able to hide from the RCMP as they likely think they can. Leo and Hatch are dialed in on this, canvassing the area and keeping a close eye on who's coming and going. I know most of his face wasn't visible, but I didn't immediately recognize the man who attacked you, so I'm confident he's not from around here…but after two days of attempts to come after you, he's got to be staying someplace close and using a reliable vehicle for transportation. We'll be checking the nearby motels and car rental facilities. One way or another, we'll smoke him out."

"Or maybe he'll give up," Cally murmured. "Three failures is a lot of wasted effort. There's got to be an easier way to make some fast cash than coming after me. I'm nobody. I haven't been somebody for a very long time."

Her voice hitched as she spoke, and Aaron's insides tightened. "I'm sure that's not true. You're someone to me, to Ellen…and I'm sure there are friends back home who feel the same way. And not to lecture, since it's none of my business, but I can almost guarantee you're somebody to your family, even if they have a terrible way of showing it." When she grew silent and unresponsive, he continued. "Er, I apologize. I didn't mean to sound patronizing. I think you have every right to be upset about recent events, and the RCMP will do everything we can to catch this criminal and set things right. Hopefully fast enough that you can enjoy the holidays without fear."

"Is that likely?"

Aaron grunted. The snow was accumulating on the front windshield faster than the wipers could brush it off. It was going to be a tricky drive. "It really depends on a number of factors, so while I don't want to tell you it's impossible, I also don't want to give you false hope."

"Fair enough."

The wheels of the patrol car slid slightly as Aaron tried to maneuver around a pile of last night's snow that the plows hadn't fully pushed onto the road's shoulder. He regained control without much trouble, but the slippery surface of the road was concerning. Keeping the wheel steady was proving to be more difficult than he'd anticipated, a sign that there was potentially black ice on the road under the thick, fresh snow. As he drove, more snow sprayed up over the front windshield and his stomach lurched. The plows hadn't been through recently, either, and judging by the way the new snow blew up and over the car, the accumulation on the road was now higher than the space underneath their vehicle. Their front bumper was working like a plow, and they still had at least another kilometer to go before reaching town.

Cally gasped as the next turn caused the car's back wheels to swing toward the center of the road. Aaron cranked the steering wheel to pull them the opposite direction, but he'd misjudged the amount of force needed and the vehicle overcorrected, sending them sliding the other way. Aaron gritted his teeth and slammed the brakes, letting the automatic braking system do its job. He'd driven on his fair share of icy, snowy roads—and even taken special driving courses on winter driving—

but the number one rule about driving in this part of Canada in the winter was to be prepared for anything.

He was more worried about the fright on Cally's face as the patrol car continued to slide sideways along the road, mercifully remaining more or less central on the roadway as they spun around in two full rotations before coming to a stop pointed the wrong way, the back end and front end in different lanes.

"We're all right," he said, reaching over to take Cally's shaking hand. "I know you're not used to Canadian winters, but I assure you that this isn't totally unusual up north."

"The snow looks so fluffy," Cally said. "Why are we sliding around? I didn't think it was slippery."

"The snow isn't what's causing the spinout, though it is what helped us stop. See how our tire tracks are cutting deep creases in the snow?" He pointed through the windshield. The snow had piled up so heavily on the road that the creases they'd cut were as deep as the wheels were high, and the top of the snow they'd driven over was marked with lines defined by the car's undercarriage. "We're hitting something called black ice. After the big snowfall yesterday, it stopped snowing and warmed up a bit this morning, which melted some of the snow. But then the second wave of the storm moved in and froze everything that melted. That's black ice, because you can't really see it on the road. And with all this other snow on top, it's literally impossible to avoid or anticipate. Sometimes it's helpful to have fresh snow, as it provides traction on the ice, but the amount of snow we have here is beyond helpful."

"Are we going to get back to town okay?" Cally twisted in her seat to look out each of the windows. "I can barely see more than a car length in front or behind us. What if someone comes barreling down the road?"

Aaron had worried about that, too, but he hadn't wanted to say anything and concern her further. "That's unlikely, since anyone else traveling this road is also going to have to drive slowly, but hopefully we'll be out of here in a minute or two..." He shifted into Reverse and pressed the gas. The engine revved and the tires spun. But they barely moved a centimeter. "That's normal for a first try. Hold tight, we just need to work our way out of here."

He shifted to Drive, moving another centimeter or so, then back to Reverse and Drive again, trying to rock the car out of its stuck position. After several minutes, however, his patience began to wane. They'd made little progress and he was beginning to worry that the patrol car was well and truly wedged in place. The accumulation in the center of the road had been greater than in the lanes, thanks to the plows likely doing a rush job the night before and pushing the snow to the road's outer lanes and the center instead of fully clearing it off.

He tried to offer Cally an encouraging smile as he opened the car door—which required some force, as he had to clear away a swath of snow to get it open—and climbed out to look underneath the vehicle.

The snow was packed hard, and several large chunks of ice that had probably fallen off vehicle tire wells and been plowed up with the snow were wedged firmly under the car near the gas tank and tailpipe. Reality sunk in as he got back into the car and tried to call up the police station on the radio.

"What's going on? Should we get out?" Cally asked.

Aaron shook his head, and his jaw tightened at the static over the car radio. None of the channels seemed to be working—there was too much interference. His cell phone signal was also nonexistent, though that was no surprise. After several minutes of failed attempts at communication, he rested his head against the seat to consider their options.

"Aaron? I'd really appreciate an update."

He had to tell her. They were going to need to work through this together. "We're well and truly stuck. If we try to push the car out, we risk damaging the underside of the vehicle—which I might be willing to try regardless, if I thought there was a possibility of success."

"So let's try it."

He stared at her. The woman was already shivering, even all bundled up in her layers. "Are you sure?"

She nodded resolutely. "You push, I'll work the gas. I mean, what's our other option? Sitting here in the cold for hours until the storm lets up and we can be rescued?"

"That, or we walk. I have an emergency blanket in the trunk that you're welcome to use. It's cold out there, but not as cold as it'll be once the sun goes down in a few hours. Then we'll be risking frostbite, but it's not nearly that frigid right now."

Cally didn't hesitate and tried to shove open the passenger door. She grunted as the metal plowed a semicircle through the snow beside the car. "Well, what are we waiting for? Let's give it a try."

Incredulous, Aaron complied and abdicated the driver's seat to Cally. She followed his shouted instructions to shift into Reverse and hit the gas as he pushed against the front end of the car, tried to dig out the wheels, then tried pushing again. It wasn't long before his muscles began to tighten and the sweat on his skin from the exertion turned cold and sent a deep chill into his bones. He grabbed the emergency kit from the trunk and rejoined Cally inside.

"So that's that, I guess," Cally murmured. "We're walking into town."

Aaron pulled out the blanket, extra gloves and scarf from the emergency kit, as well as a hot pack that could be cracked to activate. "That's our next option, yes. But I only want to walk if you're okay with it. Like I said, I think we're about a kilometer out of town, so it shouldn't take us more than a half hour to forty minutes with this weather. The hardest part will be trudging through with the snow blowing on our faces. When the breeze hits, it's chilling, and I know you're not from a cold climate."

Cally huffed as she pulled the extra gloves over her hands and wrapped a second scarf around her face. "It's not like I've never seen snow before. I went to college in Toronto. I was much younger then and really only stayed on campus during the winter, but I've seen it before. That was actually where I first met my…"

Her voice trailed off. Aaron had a feeling he knew what she'd been about to say, and he ached with sadness for her.

"Sorry," she said after a moment. She cleared her throat and blinked up at him, redness rimming her eyes but determination setting her jaw. "I think we're as bundled up as we can get. Shall we go?"

After the first ten minutes of walking, Cally wondered what they'd gotten into. After twenty minutes, she wished she'd chosen the option to stay inside the police car. Did Aaron even know if they were heading in the right direction? Her legs ached from the effort of trudging through the snow—her quadriceps felt like they were on fire. The one strange upside was that her body had warmed up enough from the exertion that she was sweating inside her winter coat—despite her face and extremities still feeling like icicles. It was the strangest sensation.

How do people live like this up here?

To her relief, they finally passed the welcome sign for the town. But as she pulled up alongside Aaron to remark on their progress, she was suddenly startled by the sight of the man beside her and found the words caught in her throat. Aaron led the way with a calm ease, willingly carving a path for her and constantly checking to ensure she stayed directly behind him so that he could take the full brunt of the cold wind and blowing snow. He looked confident and assured. A tiny flutter stirred inside her stomach.

Where is that coming from?

Why wasn't he married yet? If she knew him better— and perhaps if they weren't trudging through a snowstorm after a series of bizarre attacks by a possible kidnapper— she might ask him. She thought she still might, after they reached the station and warmed up, because the curiosity was a little overwhelming. Aaron was a serious catch for any woman, the way she saw it. Secure career, good family, loved by the community—or so she gathered from the interactions she'd seen so far—and exceptionally handsome. He and his brother Leo shared the same strong, square jawline and short, dark hair, though Aaron wore his even shorter, and his eyes were a lighter brown than his brother's. Almost more hazel than brown—not that she'd noticed for any reason beyond a matter-of-fact observation, of course.

She was also lying to herself, and she knew it. Escaping the guilt, on the other hand, was an impossible task. Plus, they lived in different countries.

"Cally? Are you all right?"

Cally looked up to find Aaron watching her with concern. Her cheeks warmed. "Yes, sorry. I'm fine. Just lost in thought."

"The swirling snow will do that to you. I can't tell you how many times I've been driving through a blizzard and had to shake myself out of a spiraling thought pattern. Look, we've reached the edge of town!" He pulled a cell phone out of his pocket, sighed and put it back. "Still no signal. Well, the RCMP station is on the other side, so we don't have that much farther to go, but it's still a small hike."

"Lead on," she said, trying very hard not to look at him. It felt like her thoughts were written clear across her face.

As they started walking again, the outlines of buildings on either side of the street became a touch clearer, though Fort Mason as a whole looked like an abandoned town. There were no cars in the streets, and no one walked around outside. The sparkle of holiday decorations on the light posts and sidewalk trees had been dulled by accumulated snow, making them look worn and tired. Cally thought back to Leo's comment on Fort Mason during the winter, how many residents either went south for a few months or stayed indoors most of the time. She supposed it was even worse than usual right now, in the middle of a snowstorm.

She was about to remark on the eerie serenity of the town when movement at the edge of her vision caught her attention. When she turned to look, she saw a hooded figure in white duck into an alley between two retail stores. Alarm punched into her stomach, but she shoved it away just as quickly. It was ridiculous to get worked up about every single person she saw wearing full-coverage clothing. The poor individual was probably just trying to get from point A to point B without freezing to death, so of course they'd have their head and body covered as much as possible.

But several minutes later, a sensation of discomfort washed over her, like she was being watched. It was the same feeling she'd had during her spa tour. When she turned her head to check, hoping it was simply her mind playing tricks on her, she once again made out the shadowy outline of a person ducking between buildings.

Was that the *same* person? It couldn't be.

"Aaron?" She tapped his shoulder and he paused, turning around. "Have you noticed anyone else outside since we've been walking?"

He shook his head. "No, we seem to be the only people outdoors. None of these shops are even open today. Why, have you?"

"Maybe I'm seeing things, but I thought I saw someone slip between the stores back there. Once about five minutes ago, and then again just now."

He frowned. "I'd like to say we don't need to worry about it, but after all that's happened, I'm not taking any chances. Come on, let's get off the main drag."

He led them down the next street, taking a shortcut through a small parking lot and around the block before meeting back up with the main street again. The moment they walked up to the corner, Cally gasped. The shadowy shape was back, and it appeared to be a person leaning against a wall under a store awning— not a trick of the light or her mind making shapes out of the falling snow. It looked as though the person was waiting for something. Or some*one*.

"Aaron…" Cally couldn't stop her voice from wavering.

"I see him," Aaron said in a low tone. "Come on, we're almost to the station. If we hurry—"

But as they took the first steps to resume their journey, Cally couldn't resist the urge to look over her shoulder.

She almost screamed.

The white-clad figure had started moving, and the person was running straight for them.

SEVEN

Aaron heard Cally's soft gasp and glanced back. Alarm and frustration flared in his gut. Could they not catch a break? This person was heading their direction at a rapid clip, and if Cally was right and they'd been followed as they trekked through town, the individual was unlikely to be running at them in order to offer a ride or a kind word for the holidays. The fact that the person hadn't said anything to introduce him or herself told Aaron all he needed to know.

They needed to hide, and fast—because there was no way they'd make it to the station before their pursuer caught up.

"This way," Aaron said. He ushered Cally around the side of a building and they ran down an alleyway, weaving around trash cans and recycle bins. Once they'd reached the back of the building, he led Cally down the narrow backstreet for delivery vehicles, heading toward the closest place he knew of where they'd be able to find shelter, even closer than the police station—the grocery store on King Street where his mother worked as an occasional merchandiser and food sample demonstrator. More than once, he'd helped

his mother bring her boxes of product into the store before it opened for the day, so he knew the security code
to get inside via the stockroom entrance.

*Thank You, Lord! Your provision never ceases to
amaze me.*

They rushed up to the door. Aaron fumbled to remove his glove and lift the protective lid from the security pad.

"He's in the alleyway." Cally's voice cracked. "Aaron?"

His fingers, cramped from the cold, refused to do
what his brain was telling them to. He had to hold his
right hand steady with his left, guiding his fingers to
punch in the numbers on the pad, all the while praying that the code hadn't been changed since the last
time he'd visited.

The white-clad figure was close enough for Aaron to
see that he or she wore a heavy white winter coat and
a ski mask over the face—a getup similar to the one
worn by the attacker at Cally's cabin, but the coat was
a new addition, as opposed to the plain white hoodie
from the cabin. The person also wore heavier boots
than the man at the spa. Footsteps thumped the ground
with every step. *Was the attacker at the spa a different
person than the intruder at the cabin? What about the
attacker in black at the airport?*

It didn't make sense, but he wasn't going to wait
around to ask questions. The metallic click of a sliding lock brought a wave of relief, and he pushed the
door open to usher Cally inside. He slipped in behind
her, slammed the door closed and slid the manual interior lock into place just as a heavy object thumped
against the metal.

Cally screamed and jumped, and Aaron flinched

back in surprise. The handle rattled as the person outside tried the door. The manual lock shook, too, which worried Aaron more than he wanted it to.

"Can you use the electronic lock again?" Cally said, backing deeper into the stockroom. "That doesn't sound very sturdy."

"It'll hold," Aaron said with more confidence than he felt. "It's old, but it'll hold. I'm afraid I don't know the code to lock back up—I've only ever come here before opening. Let's not stay, though. There should be a landline somewhere in the store that we can use to call the station for backup. Let's go."

He wrapped his arm around Cally's shoulders to lead them into the main area of the store, but as soon as they crossed the threshold from the stockroom, Aaron pulled them to a halt. He'd forgotten that the entire front of the grocery store was made up of large glass windows. And while they could hardly see anything outside of the windows thanks to the snowstorm—the stores on the other side were totally obscured—anyone could walk by and peer in. He'd been thinking he might turn on the lights so they could navigate the store better, but the curtainless windows ruled that right out.

"Where should we search for the phone?" Cally whispered.

The rattling at the back door stopped as Aaron squinted into the darkened store. "The manager's office should have a phone. Maybe the customer service desk, too." He waved her along the back aisle, behind the shelving units. Faint light from the freezers illuminated the way enough that they could see where they were going without banging into things.

They reached the door to the manager's office and Aaron turned the knob. It was locked.

"The customer service desk is up near the front," he said, heading down the next closest aisle.

He froze as a blurry shape moved in front of the window.

"Go back!" He gestured at Cally to back up to the far end of the aisle. They stood with their backs to a display of soup cans, and Aaron prayed that their reflection in the security mirrors mounted around the corners of the store's ceiling wouldn't be visible to the person outside. He peered around the edge of the aisle. The person dressed in white was walking slowly past the broad windows. If Aaron tried to reach the customer service desk, he'd be spotted. He pulled out his phone again, hoping the signal had returned. It hadn't.

Cally exclaimed something in what he figured was Amaran before sighing in frustration. "Why don't they just give up? Clearly I'm not an easy target. I'm being protected by armed law enforcement—they're not going to win if this turns even more serious."

"I appreciate your faith in me. And if I have to, I'll use my Taser or sidearm, but I'm hoping the situation won't come to that." Aaron looked around the shelves again. The person was gone—or at least no longer visible. For all he knew, the individual might be waiting at the edge of the windows, peering around to look at them the same way Aaron was looking for him. Or her.

Aaron couldn't say for sure if this was the same attacker as at the spa, but if so, he had to be using a highly reliable form of transportation to be able to move from one place to another so quickly. Otherwise, how had they all made it into town at the same time?

There'd been no other tire tracks on the road into town. Even if the tracks had been covered by snow, this person's car would have certainly been stuck, too... It wasn't as though he and Cally had left much later than the fleeing attacker.

Were there actually two people involved? Maybe Aaron had read the man's expression wrong during their face-off at the spa. Regardless, Fort Mason was a small town—this person or these people wouldn't be able to hide for long. And for that matter, certainly the attacker or attackers knew that Aaron was an RCMP officer, and still they'd gone after Cally. Twice prior while he was in uniform—three times if he counted this incident, since he was still wearing his gear despite technically being off the clock. This culprit was either incredibly brave or very unwise.

Or totally clueless.

"I'm going to make a break for the customer service desk," Aaron said. "Our options here are to sit and wait for cell service or to make a landline call out, and I'm not content to just sit here. I can defend us if necessary, but as an RCMP officer, I need to disengage as much as possible."

Cally took a deep breath and exhaled slowly. "Do you think they're going to find another way in? There's not another door we're unaware of, is there?"

"Like at the cabin? No. I don't think so. But I'd advise you to stay here and keep low to the ground, okay? Stay out of the way while I make the call. Backup should get here in minutes—or faster."

Cally frowned but nodded in support. Part of him wanted to wait a moment longer, to say something to reassure her that everything happening had to be a huge misunderstanding, but he couldn't bring himself to say words he didn't fully believe. He'd be setting a bad example as a leader if he willingly offered false hope. But if he kept her expectations realistic and brought them out of this peacefully and uninjured, it'd look good on his record. First and foremost, however, he'd have done his job honestly and well.

He crouched and turned around to face the direction of the customer service desk. He didn't want to spend time unlatching the small gate at the desk, but his other option was to hoist himself over the countertop and drop into the center of the customer service space.

The longer he waited, the more he'd get inside his own head—so he counted to three and sprang out from the hiding spot. He bounded across the store without anyone in sight outside.

Less than three meters from the desk, the figure dressed in white appeared at the window. Aaron's stomach lurched in surprise, but he kept moving. The figure stopped in a wide-legged stance and reached for something at their waist.

Aaron's fingers touched the edge of the customer service desk's countertop, and he made a decision—he gripped it and launched himself over the side, spotting the phone immediately. He grabbed the entire handset and pulled it down into the central well of the desk, then dialed the station directly. The click of his call being answered came within seconds.

"Requesting assistance at the Grocery Mart. I repeat, we have an emergency at the Grocery Mart, needing backup immediately."

"Aaron?" Leo's voice was incredulous. "You've got it. Is the perp armed?"

"Unsure."

"On our way."

Aaron dropped the phone and started to stand, but the instant his head crested the top of the customer service desk, he dropped down again.

A bang split the air, and the front window of the grocery store shattered as the figure in white fired at Aaron's hiding space.

Please, Lord. Keep Cally safe.

He hoped she'd stay quiet and make her way to the back room. There were boxes to hide behind or inside until the cavalry arrived. He could already hear sirens. He also heard the secondary smash of window shards being knocked out of the way so that someone could enter over the windowsill without slicing themselves open. What was with this person and smashing windows?

Aaron reached for his sidearm—then thought better of it and chose his stun weapon instead. He didn't know exactly where in the building Cally had holed up, and he didn't want to take the risk of shooting toward the shelves with real bullets. Carefully and quietly, he slid his Taser out of the holster. As long as the individual remained focused on Aaron's hiding space and not Cally, Aaron was confident he could hold the person off with his stun weapon until backup arrived. The sirens were already growing louder, but the footsteps still came closer, crunching on the broken glass.

And then he heard the thump of an overturned box. The footsteps stopped. Glass scraped.

The footsteps took off in another direction.

Aaron didn't waste a moment. He leaped over the customer service desk, Taser at the ready. He raced after the intruder as Cally suddenly cried out. Flashing lights were visible in the falling snow as Aaron ran past the windows.

"Stop! RCMP!" Aaron shouted, seeing the intruder disappear into the back room.

Seconds later there was another bang.

Cally's screams went silent.

Cally scurried backward in the darkness of the stockroom, weaving around boxes and under shelving as the intruder advanced on her hiding place. An empty box had fallen as she'd come into the room, surprising her so much that she'd accidentally cried out. Now, the intruder's head swiveled side to side as if trying to figure out where she'd gone, and there was no mistaking the shiny black object in his hands.

Why am I being shot at?

She filled her lungs, readying a scream for help, when the whoop of a siren sounded outside. The intruder took two steps toward where she'd crouched behind a pile of crates, then seemed to think better of it and ran at the back exit, slamming a shoulder into the metal door. The loose manual bolt, which she'd been worried about earlier, came free and crashed to the floor with a bang. The intruder went sprawling outside, and the stockroom door swung closed.

She almost cried from the intensity of her relief. If she still talked to God, she'd thank Him for keeping her safe…but she couldn't bring herself to do it. Was her anger justified? She wasn't sure. She knew the Book of Job inside and out and was well aware that sometimes tragedies happened for God's greater purpose, even if it was impossible to understand at the time—and even if it hurt terribly—and she also knew that feeling bitter and angry toward God was a dangerous state to be in. Would she ever blame God for taking Esai away from her? She had at first, even if she hadn't said it aloud. She'd known intellectually that it wasn't God's fault, but that didn't make it hurt any less.

Aaron burst into the stockroom, his own weapon drawn. "Cally! Where are you?"

Without waiting for an answer, he crossed to the back door that was swinging shut and poked his head out.

"I'm over here!" She stood as Aaron rushed forward and reached out as if he wanted to hug her. At the last moment, he pulled his arm back. "Are you hurt? I heard a bang. It sounded like a shot went off."

"It was the door," she said, pointing at it. "See the sliding latch? It's on the floor. I had a bad feeling about that latch when it was rattling. Good thing the store has upgraded to the electronic security, but they might want to replace that."

"Agreed." Aaron guided her back to the front of the store where two RCMP vehicles waited, then sent the other officers on the hunt for the intruder. Cally had a feeling they wouldn't get far, though. The snow, while it had eased up somewhat, still fell heavily, obscuring everyone's vision and covering up footprints. "Let's get moving. The station is a block and a half down the road."

She eyed the road. It looked like there'd been an attempt at plowing it since the morning. It wasn't totally clear, but far better than the highway. "Are we walking?"

Aaron shook his head. "Not while there's someone

out there searching for you, we're not. Leo is fine for us to take his car back. I don't want to keep you outside any longer than you've already been."

They got into the vehicle. Aaron drove carefully down the road, and Cally's body began to relax as she anticipated a chance to sit in a warm building with a hot beverage and no chance of being attacked.

Or at least, she hoped not—she'd already been wrong about that yesterday. *Twice.*

EIGHT

Cally sat in the staff room at the RCMP station with a steaming mug of tea between her hands and a space heater blowing hot air directly on her legs. Aaron slid into the seat across from her. He had a stack of paperwork in his arms, and for the first time that day, Cally noticed the dark circles under his eyes.

"You need anything else, let one of us know, okay? We can set up a quiet space in one of the offices if you want to try getting some rest. Don't hesitate to ask."

Cally stared at the blank wall on the other side of the staff room. She'd wanted a change of scenery, and now she had it—and honestly, her life hadn't been full of this much excitement in a very long time. Not that being stalked and attacked was the kind of excitement she was looking for. It was a good thing these events were happening in a small town, though. If her mother found out what was going on, Cally would never hear the end of it. The guilt and pressure to come home would be unrelenting.

But did she even *want* to stay here? The longer she remained at Fort Mason, the more she monopolized Aaron's time. This couldn't be how he wanted to spend what was supposed to be a quiet, low-stress period at his job, either. "I'm sorry," she finally said, resting her head in her hands. "You've probably got a million other things you'd rather be doing than babysitting a grown woman."

Aaron pressed his lips together, looking sheepish. "Honestly? I don't mind. It gets a little lonely around here this time of year. And besides…" His voice trailed off and he sighed. "This is my job, you know? And your visit, uh—"

"I'm an assignment." She remembered the phrasing of the email she'd received. *Foreign dignitary. Personal concierge.* "I get it, but you don't have to pretend. And I'm a fully capable adult. I can handle myself if there are other things you have to do. Ellen can take over as my hangout buddy when she gets here."

"Which might not be until tomorrow, and with these multiple attempts on your life, it's not exactly a matter of just hanging out. I know you know that. Also, I think she'll be a little too preoccupied with wedding stuff, right?"

Cally shrugged. "I'll be out of your way soon enough." She realized how negative that sounded as soon as the words left her mouth. He'd done the best he could to look out for her, and she didn't mean to sound ungrateful. "I'll be somebody else's problem," she tried instead. Nope, that was worse.

He blinked slowly at her, fingers rubbing the sides of his temples. He looked bewildered and ready to topple over from exhaustion at any moment. Guilt washed over her—again, she'd been retreating into self-pity instead of paying attention to the people around her. Was she so incapable of considering others' feelings?

"Aaron? Do you think maybe you should get some more rest?"

He grunted and rubbed his eyes. "I'll rest when there's time for it, and right now, there isn't. With Leo and Hatch out searching for the intruder, that leaves me to man the station and look out for you."

She frowned. "There's no one else you can call in for a few hours? An emergency volunteer or auxiliary officer?"

He shook his head. "We're low-staffed at this time of year—not that there are many of us here year-round. It's my brothers and I, Hatch and our part-time recep-tionist. If we have a big emergency, we can usually call up some extra help from Fort St. Jacob, but with the roads the way they are right now, it's just not possible."

The memory of trudging through the snow made Cally shiver and wrap the blanket draped around her shoulders a little tighter. "But what about people out on the roads? Or if there's an emergency at someone's house?"

Aaron chuckled, but the sound lacked humor. "I promise you that things are not usually so frantic in Fort Mason. In my entire time working here, we've only had one large winter storm emergency, and that was because the snow brought in a ton of ice and caused one of the large trees at the edge of town to topple over. It took down power lines, which lit the hardware store on fire and injured three people. Most of Fort Mason didn't have power for a week, and that's a scary thing up here with minus twenty-five Celsius the average temperature this time of year. The trucks couldn't get up to fix our infrastructure and repair the power lines… It was a total mess.

"But never anything like shootings or stalkers, or… well, that's not quite true. I think I mentioned there was an incident with my brother earlier this year, but that's another story entirely, and it happened in the spring. And then my other brother got involved in a scary homicide case around Fort St. Jacob, but that's a few hours south of here and it was in May, not winter, so…where was I going with this?"

Cally couldn't resist the urge to smile. He was definitely beyond exhausted. She recognized it in the over-exaggerated gestures and the way he'd started to ramble. But he was trying very hard to continue to protect her and do the best job possible, and she appreciated it. "You were telling me why you can't take a nap. Are you sure you can't lie down in one of the back rooms while I monitor the front area? You didn't sleep last night, and the longer you go without rest, the less effective you'll be on the job. It's not like an attacker is going to waltz into the RCMP station and start shooting. You have cameras everywhere, and they'd be caught immediately."

"That's true. We have a lockdown protocol. But I honestly can't sleep on the clock when I'm the only officer in the building. I did have that quick nap at the spa before we left, remember? And even if you were looking out for me, if anyone found out it'd compromise my job, and if that happened, I'd be taken right out of the running for any promotions. Not that I'm going to still be in the running after the spectacular failure this assignment has been…"

Cally frowned, wanting to ask him to clarify what he meant, but his eyes had closed.

She let Aaron sit there with his eyes shut for several minutes, acting like nothing unusual had happened in case there were security cameras in the staff room. The part of her that was trying not to wallow in self-pity wanted to convert her emotions into anger and redirect the blame—but blaming Aaron or the town would get her nowhere. In theory, this could be happening anywhere—even back home in Amar, and there she had no one who'd rally around her to keep her safe, despite Aaron's insistence otherwise. Her family would complain that she'd married outside her station and brought her trouble on herself, and then they'd attempt to match her up with some random man her aunt knew or her mother had met at sewing club, or someone's cousin's brother's best friend remembered from a church dinner party.

Cally startled as her phone vibrated inside her sweater. After being without cell service all morning, she'd forgotten about checking for messages or phone calls. When she pulled the device out of her pocket, her mother's photo flashed across the screen.

She didn't want to answer it. Then again, she couldn't avoid her family forever. And after the events of today, she was feeling a little anxious about the fragility of life.

"Hi, Mama." She braced herself for the scolding. Her mother alone had left about six or seven messages on her phone since she'd left Amar, but Cally hadn't had the chance to return a single one.

"Callandra Leah Roslin, where are you and when are you coming home? What on earth has gotten into you?"

Her mother continued to rant for several minutes, and Cally listened quietly while her mother got it out of her system. Across the table, Aaron opened his eyes, yawned and flipped through the papers in front of him with slow, languid movements. The man looked set to keel over at any moment.

When her mother paused for a breath, Cally jumped in. "Are you quite finished? I love you, Mama, but I think sometimes you forget that I'm an adult. I'm in my thirties, not thirteen."

"You mean thirty-two going on thirteen, because a real adult wouldn't abandon her mother at Christmas and disappear to the other side of the world without a single thought for her family—"

"First, Uncle Zarek flies around the world at holidays and no one bats an eye, and second, I didn't abandon anyone. I can go wherever I want, whenever I want, and I don't need to provide you with a full itinerary. I left you a message that I was leaving and why, so I'm not sure what else you want from me."

Her mother scoffed. "You could have done *more* than send a measly text message. I thought you might be dead by the side of the road. Your aunt Tamara thought she heard something about a plane crash in Canada, and your uncle Zarek is concerned that you didn't contact him first since he's already in Canada for some annual conference he attends. I told everyone there's no way you're missing Christmas with the family. Esai made you do that one too many times and we were all sick of it, and now you don't have to miss the holidays anymore. Right? Tell me you're getting on a plane right now."

Cally loved her mother, she really did. But if she heard one more disparaging comment about her late husband, she was going to explode. This was the reason she hadn't felt bad about up and leaving on short notice, and besides, she really did have a marvelous reason—her friend was getting married, and she wanted to celebrate with her! And yes, she'd missed a few family Christmases for Esai's work trips—he'd been a high-profile technology consultant, and sometimes that required him to be gone during the holiday season. Rather than let him spend the holidays alone in a strange place, she'd gone with him on those occasions and been happy to do so. But her family had resented it, and apparently still did. They'd never liked him, and it had only become more difficult to manage their feelings on the matter after his death.

For once, she wanted to spend Christmas with people she knew wouldn't disparage her life choices and who'd let her grieve and love in her own way.

"I'm not getting on a plane, Mama. I'm sorry that it upsets you, but I promise I'm fine and I'll visit you as soon as I return. No, I don't know when that is, but sometime after my friend Ellen's wedding, which I've already told you about." She braced herself for the onslaught of questions about the wedding and the inevitable recommendation that she remarry someone the family approved of this time, but unlike previous rants she'd endured, Cally felt oddly calm during this one.

Yes, she'd been attacked and shot at multiple times in the past twenty-four hours…but the man across from her at the table was going above and beyond the call of duty to ensure that she didn't get hurt and to make her comfortable despite the series of events. Even as he sat half-asleep at the table, clearly on the verge of collapse, he refused to take a short break.

On the other hand, being around Aaron felt inexplicably natural, and she was struck by a pang of sadness for the loss of moments like this in her life. Would she ever have them again? If she did, she'd want these small, shared moments to be with someone like Aaron—someone dedicated and hardworking in his career, but also compassionate and caring enough to balance family, even in the midst of crisis.

"Callandra? Are you listening?"

"Yes, Mama. I'm listening. And I'm sorry I can't be everywhere and do everything at once, but I promise you I'll have a wonderful Christmas here in Fort Mason, and you'll have a wonderful holiday at home with everyone else. You won't even notice my absence once the festivities pick up."

"I very much doubt that, but…" Her mother sighed pointedly. "Are you safe? What about that plane crash your aunt mentioned?"

Cally wasn't very well going to lie to her mother, but she also didn't want to give her greater reason to worry. "There's no plane crash in this area. Canada is a big place. There's a bad snowstorm here and I didn't have cell reception for a while, and I've run into a little trouble, but please don't be concerned. I'm being looked out for by a very capable RCMP officer. He's the head of his detachment and knows what he's doing."

"Trouble! What kind of trouble?" Her mother paused for a moment on the other end of the line. "Wait, did you say an RCMP officer? Is he married?"

Cally groaned, earning a look of surprise from Aaron. Her mother's voice coming through the receiver wasn't exactly quiet. She shrugged and mouthed "Sorry!" before answering. "Mama, I'm not having this conversation with you right now."

After a few more prying questions, she managed to get off the phone, earning a curious look from Aaron.

She sighed. "Yes, my mother talks a lot. And she asks a lot of questions. She's always been a worrier and too into other people's business, but that's my entire family for you."

Aaron grinned and leaned back in his chair. "I'm getting a clearer picture of what you meant when you said you came here to try to escape them. No wonder you flew all the way to the middle of nowhere instead of landing on a tropical island or visiting a big, bustling city."

"Right? And that's only part of it. I also didn't want to endure another holiday season where they disparage the memory of my late husband and try to set me up with random men I'm not interested in. They're looking out for me in their own way, I get it, but it's overwhelming at times. I just want a chance to enjoy the holidays with zero expectations. Figure myself out again, you know? I have the wedding to attend, of course, but that's just one day, and that's going to be a happy affair."

Aaron's smile slid from his face and he leaned in. "I don't mean to pry—and please don't take this the wrong way—but will you be okay? At the wedding?"

Cally smiled despite the sadness behind the question. "Yes. I'll be all right. I'm thrilled for Ellen, and it's not like I'm bitter or don't believe in love anymore. What happened to Esai was tragic and unexpected, and I'll never stop loving him. But I'm also not going to stop living my life. He wouldn't want me to. I wouldn't want him to if our situations had been reversed. If anything, it's forced me to confront my own mortality. I don't want to waste the time I've been given."

She'd never spoken those words aloud, and hearing them from her own lips brought a wave of emotion. Without warning, tears fell from her eyes, but she didn't feel upset or overcome with sadness—rather, she felt a surge of relief to have admitted those things out loud. To finally give voice to the way she'd been feeling lately.

She touched her locket beneath her sweater, but pulled her hand away almost immediately, feeling self-conscious about the gesture with Aaron's eyes on her.

After everything she'd just confessed, she hoped Aaron didn't think badly of her—but when she looked up to meet his eyes, his smile had returned, kind and gentle.

"That makes perfect sense," he said, sliding out from his seat and into the chair next to her. "Can I see it? The locket? It's okay if you don't want to show me."

She hesitated, her first instinct being to retreat inward, like when her family brought up her past—but Aaron didn't speak begrudgingly or with sarcasm. His voice held sincerity, genuine interest in someone who'd meant so much to her. She pulled the chain from beneath her shirt and opened the locket, holding it out to him on her palm. He had to lean in to take a closer look, and she instinctively braced herself for a pitying look that never came.

"Handsome fellow," Aaron said, gazing up at her with a twinkle in his eye. "I'm glad you had someone in your life who made you smile like that."

The burden on her heart lifted, ever so slightly. "Thank you for saying so." She closed the pendant and slipped it back under her collar, the cooled metal against her skin a welcome reminder of its precious value. "My uncle did a fantastic job choosing the photo to put inside. I'm very grateful that at least *someone* in my family isn't constantly in my face about the way life has gone for me."

Aaron sat back in his chair, thoughtful. "For what it's worth—"

Before he could finish his comment, a loud popping noise came from all around them. The lights went out and the rumble of the building's heating system dropped into silence. Surprise shot through Cally at the sudden loss of light and sound, but moments later, the fluorescent lights flickered on overhead as a thump and a buzz indicated that a backup power generator had kicked in.

"Great," Aaron muttered. "Probably ice and heavy snow buildup on the power lines. Or could just be here at the station—this is an old building. I'll have to go up on the roof to check the breakers."

He pulled his phone out of his pocket, but before he'd even started to dial, it rang. "Right, reception is working again. Ironic, though I should have figured it out when your call came through. Ugh, nothing makes sense during these bad storms. Hard to say what will work or stop working when." He answered his phone and hung up moments later, looking concerned.

Cally's stomach tightened. "What is it? Tell me there hasn't been another attack?"

Aaron frowned and stood, pulling his jacket back on. "Worse. There's been three."

Town citizens had made three phone calls to 911 in a matter of minutes, according to Leo. Leo was on his way to the call nearest to him, a report of a home invasion. Hatch was on his way to help with the second call, which had come from a citizen who'd foolishly taken his snowmobile out for a drive during the terrible conditions and was apparently trapped underneath a fence with a possible head and leg injury. The third call—about another possible break-in—had come from the church across the road. Power was out across the entire town. According to Leo, the woman on the other end of the phone had sounded terrified and claimed to be hiding in a storage room while she called.

Aaron hesitated to leave the police station unattended, but at the same time, there were people who needed help—and at least one individual was on the loose in town with a weapon that they weren't hesitant to use.

"I have to respond to a call," Aaron said, pulling on his gloves and heavy boots again. He shoved aside the wave of exhaustion and prayed that he'd be able to respond effectively to the 911 caller's needs despite his lack of sleep. "It's an emergency, and Leo and Hatch are already responding to emergencies elsewhere. It's a fine time for so many calls to come in, but I guess today is handing over its fair share of inconveniences."

Cally nodded and started to gather up her things. "Should I stay here? That's probably safest, right?"

Normally, he might agree with her, but these weren't normal circumstances. With the power out and the station operating on an emergency backup generator, station security was compromised. Leaving Cally in an area where he wasn't 100 percent sure of the security was not a mistake he was willing to make again. After all, the spa was supposed to be secured, and yet an intruder had managed to get inside. And even with all the doors locked at the grocery store, the attacker had forced his way inside by shooting the glass.

Not to mention that as a foreign citizen, there could be certain legalities involved in leaving Cally alone and unattended in what was technically a government building. "I know this is normally the most secure place in town, but with the system mostly down, I'm not comfortable leaving you here alone. There are potential legal issues, too, so we need another option."

"Isn't there another place you can stash me in here that's specially locked? It wouldn't be for a long time, right?"

He sighed, liking this less and less. He needed to make a fast decision and get over to the church to respond to the emergency call. "It shouldn't be, but the town is still dealing with the fallout of the storm, and there's always a possibility that either myself or the other officers will get held up. Honestly, I think the safest place for you is in a patrol car. The glass is bulletproof and—"

Cally gathered up her bag and began slipping on her coat and boots. "You've got an emergency to respond to and I'm holding you up. You can bring me right back here after it's all done, but in the meantime you'll know exactly where I am and can keep an eye on me. I get it. Plus, bulletproof glass is more protection than we've had anywhere else so far."

Within three minutes, they were back in the patrol car. Neither leaving Cally in the empty RCMP station nor bringing her along on a call seemed right, but he figured these were exceptional circumstances, and he could only do so much while Fort Mason was short-staffed. But as Aaron pressed the keypad to lock the police station, the emergency lights inside the building flickered and died, plunging the area into murky gray twilight. Daylight was already fading outside, and it wouldn't be long before they had to sit inside the station in the dark with plummeting temperatures outside *and* inside.

Aaron sighed. "Guess bringing you along is the right call after all. I'm thinking snow must have accumulated on a transformer. If it's not fixed when we get back, I can take a look and see if it's something we can repair ourselves—or at least find a way to get the generator back up and running again."

Within minutes, Aaron had pulled up in front of the church. The lights along the front were out, giving the building a foreboding appearance as twilight deepened. With only six hours of full daylight at this time of year, night came quickly and made everything look dark and mysterious. He started to open his door, then glanced back at Cally.

"Stay in here, okay? You're safest inside this car, and I'll be just inside the church. If for any reason you need help, use this radio right here. I've set it to the same frequency as my radio, so call me first before reacting. If I don't respond immediately, it might mean there's something happening inside. Keep trying."

Cally nodded, her eyes wide. "Be safe."

His return smile was tight, and he was hit with a wave of nausea as he exited the car and stepped with caution up the front stairs. Leaving her behind was the last thing he wanted to do, but it really was the safest choice.

He knocked on the church door and announced himself, but when no one answered, he pressed on the front door. It swung open into a darkened foyer. He pulled out his flashlight and held it out, searching for the light switch. It wasn't hard to find, but the power was out in the church, too. He swung the flashlight back and forth instead, seeing nothing but an empty entrance space.

The sanctuary looked just as abandoned, but he wasn't all that surprised—especially if the person who'd called was hiding in a storage room, thinking someone was still skulking around the church.

"Hello? Anyone here? I'm RCMP Officer Aaron Thrace." He called into each room as he passed, his anxiety growing with every moment. All the rooms he encountered were dark, and no one responded to his calls. After several minutes, he'd checked every room he could think of and found no one. There wasn't even an open door anywhere, aside from the front door that had been open when he arrived. He'd descended into the basement to check the rooms downstairs when his walkie-talkie buzzed.

He picked it up, hoping for good news. "Aaron here."

"Hey, it's Leo. Are you at the 911 call at the church?"

"Yeah." The space upstairs was beautifully decorated for Christmas, and nothing in the sanctuary had appeared to be missing. None of the offices had looked broken into, and there wasn't any sign of life down in the basement, either. Maybe someone had been hungry and stolen from the food bank donation boxes? In which case, he couldn't blame them for coming inside. He'd rather someone steal food from a donation bin than go hungry. "I haven't found anyone yet, not even the caller. I don't know if she left before I got here or if I've missed a room. It took about seven minutes to get over after you called."

"Well, that settles it." Leo sighed. "Something isn't right about this. When Hatch got to the supposed scene of the snowmobile incident, no one was there. He's double-checking the location in case he got it wrong, but I'm starting to wonder. The call at Mrs. Henderson's was a dud—I found no evidence of a break-in and she didn't remember making the call. Mind you, she doesn't remember a lot these days, but—"

A chill washed over Aaron's body. "Are you telling me that all three of us haven't found evidence for the 911 calls we received? They've all turned out to be nothing so far?"

"Yeah, I am. They can't all be fake, though. I mean—"

Fake phone calls meant occupying all of the RCMP officers in the town, isolating the one person who was actually a target.

And they'd played right into it.

NINE

Cally hunkered down inside the patrol car, wishing she'd brought a book to keep herself distracted from her own thoughts. She had a few digital magazines on her phone, but they weren't holding her interest. She alternated between reading and watching the snow outside, which fell so lightly now that it almost looked pretty—though she figured she'd be better able to appreciate its beauty if she'd hadn't spent a good chunk of the day trekking through knee-high snowdrifts. As much as she enjoyed the winter aesthetic, she'd had about enough of snow for a little while.

She closed her eyes and leaned her head against the seat. It wasn't comfortable, but it was better than sitting in a pitch-black police station and slowly turning into an icicle. Aaron had left the patrol car running so she could stay warm—and she was getting warmer by the moment. She placed her phone on the seat next to her and began to unwind her scarf, sliding off several layers of now-stifling winter gear. As a mountain of fabric accumulated on the passenger seat, she accidentally knocked her phone onto the floor. With a huff of frustration, she leaned down to grab it. Her eyes naturally drifted out the window as she sat upright.

She slapped a hand over her mouth to stifle a scream. A white-clad figure stood less than a block away, looking as though he was trying to blend into the snow-covered exterior of a brick building. Although the snow wasn't falling nearly as heavily as it had been before—so the person couldn't hide in the reduced visibility—the haze of twilight made it easier for the person to slip in and around the lengthening shadows.

She yanked her eyes away from the window. She needed to call Aaron and let him know. Her immediate instinct was to get out and run as far away as possible, but Aaron had made a strong point about the patrol car being the safest place for her. It had bulletproof windows, and she'd locked it from the inside. No one could get in unless they had the key, and no one shooting at her would hit her inside, either. She didn't actually know how many shots bulletproof glass could take before it cracked, but if someone started shooting, she had a pretty strong hunch that either Aaron or one of the other RCMP officers would hear it and come running before that happened.

Cally unlocked her phone and fumbled to hit the correct icons to call Aaron, but her fingerprints weren't registering on the device. She wiped her hand on her pants and tried again. He'd told her to use the radio, but she'd have to sit up to do that, putting her in full view through the window.

Her heart thudded in her chest and she sank down in the seat, trying to make herself as small as possible. She glanced out the car window at the place she'd last noticed the white-clad figure. The person was no longer there, and for some reason, that made her even more nervous. She took a deep breath as her call connected. Aaron answered on the first ring, but the crackle of static filled the receiver.

"Cally? What's going on?" His voice sounded distant and kept cutting out. "Why aren't you using the radio?"

"Hello? Aaron? Can you hear me?"

"Cally? I'm in the basement of the church. Is everything all right?"

"I'm not sure. I might have seen the attacker from the grocery store again. My eyes might be playing tricks on me, but someone was down the street, wearing white. I tried to keep an eye on the figure but the person disappeared. I don't know if they went inside the church, or if they've gone, or—"

A shadow crossed in front of the passenger-side window and she screamed.

"Cally? Cally! What's happening!" Aaron shouted through the phone.

Cally slipped between the seats, lowering herself onto the floor between the rear passenger seats and the back of the driver's seat. She stared at the window, her entire body beginning to shake—and then the shadow became the torso of a person dressed in white as the visitor walked around the vehicle. The driver's-side handle rattled as the intruder attempted to open it. The person tried both rear doors. Then the front passenger door. Cally kept one hand pressed against her mouth and brought the phone back up to her ear.

"He's here," she whispered. "Circling the car."

"I'm on my way," Aaron snapped. "Don't move."

She didn't plan on it. But as the person circled the car again, as if trying to figure out how to get inside,

Cally's fear shifted into something else. Anger. Frustration. Why were they bothering her? It made no sense.

In defiance, she held up the phone. "Police are almost here," she said, uncertain whether the individual would be able to hear her or not. "You're not going to get away with this much longer."

She wasn't sure if the person had heard her through the thick glass, but her visitor circled the car to stand at the opposite side from where she'd crouched between the seats—and then raised a gloved hand to point directly at her. A second gesture was a slice across the person's throat, then a hand pointing at Cally again. In that moment, she was struck by a horrifying revelation.

This person wants me dead, and won't stop until the deed is done.

"I don't know what you want from me," she cried. "I've done nothing. I'm worth nothing. Leave me alone!"

The person's hand tightened into a fist and, in a futile gesture of frustration, punched the window. The slam resounded with a painful-sounding *thunk*, and the white-suited figure backed up, shaking their hand. Cally felt a momentary surge of triumph that was almost immediately quashed when the person drew a gun out of their pocket and, without a second's hesitation, fired three rounds into the window.

Cally squeezed her arms against her chest and made herself as small as possible. The screams she heard were her own, but she couldn't stop them—and then the world fell silent, save for the echo of the bangs in her ears. She'd shut her eyes tight, unable to look, fearful that she'd glance up and see holes in the window or a cracked pane ready to cave in.

Please, God, protect me. Keep me safe, keep Aaron safe. Help us through this.

The instant she lifted up the prayer, she felt guilty. She hadn't talked to God for how long, and now here she was using Him for help? That didn't seem right.

I shouldn't talk to Him at all, she thought. *What's He going to do for me anyway?*

Footsteps crunched near the car, and a thud against the side door made her shriek in fright again. But when she opened her eyes, Aaron had unlocked the car. He slid into the back seat and closed the door. He immediately gripped her under the arms and pulled her up onto the seat proper. His voice was muffled in her ringing ears.

"Cally. Hey! Are you all right?"

His stare was intense and the most serious she'd ever seen on him. She opened her mouth to respond and found that nothing came out—and then she realized that her hands were shaking so hard that she could no longer control her movements. No, not just her hands. Her entire body was shaking, and she couldn't stop it.

"I...the gun...we..."

"Gone. The immediate danger is gone. You're safe." Aaron pulled her into a hug. He squeezed her tightly, and although she knew she was still trembling in his arms, there was a deep sense of comfort in the gesture of human contact. She couldn't remember the last time she'd been hugged like this, securely and sincerely. The utter terror she'd felt when the gun had been pointed at her began to abate.

She didn't know how long they stayed that way, but eventually Aaron released her and she sat with her head leaning against the seat, breath still coming in shallow gasps—but she no longer shook uncontrollably.

"I threatened that the police were on the way. The person got angry and shot at the window and then must have run off so as to not get caught. I'm so sorry. I should have stayed quiet. It's my fault you weren't able to catch the attacker by surprise. I know you said the glass is bulletproof," she said, talking as much to herself as to him, "but the person was right in front of me, and when that gun came out, all I could think was—"

The recollection made her shake again. Aaron pulled her toward him a second time and, most inexplicably, kissed her forehead. She reeled back in shock. His lips parted in surprise, as if he hadn't realized what he was doing.

"I'm so sorry," he said, the words fast and clipped. "I wasn't thinking. You're not a child. I shouldn't have done that."

"It's okay," she said. Truthfully, she wasn't upset—just startled at his outward show of affection.

"Look," he continued without meeting her eyes, "we're going to make our way back to the police station and get the generator back up and running until the main power comes on again. The 911 calls were all fake. A tech team in Fort St. Jacob is going to work on figuring out where they originated from, but it seems as though someone was actively trying to isolate you from law enforcement. I don't know if they intended to break into the police station or what, but this person or people are desperate to get to you."

Cally squeezed her hands into tight fists, nails digging into the flesh of her palms. "Why me? What is the point to all this? Shooting at a police car, no less!

Do they not value their own life at all? Why risk you coming out to stop them?"

Aaron didn't respond and she groaned.

"I wish there was some way to communicate. Some way to let them know I'm not worth whatever they think I am. I don't want to go through this anymore, and to be quite honest, I was personally fine until this moment, but now…I don't know why I bothered coming to Canada. I wish I'd never gotten on that plane at all. I wish I'd stayed in Amar."

Aaron's heart broke in two at Cally's admission. He listened in silence while she recounted the entirety of what had just happened as she sat in the car. Of course she was questioning why she'd come to Fort Mason— everything had gone completely wrong since the moment she stepped off the plane at the Rocky North Regional Airport. If only he'd been able to get out of the church faster, he might have been able to stop the attacker, but by the time he'd bounded up the steps from the basement, navigated through the darkened building and made it outside again, the person was gone. He might have taken off in pursuit—there were several sets of footprints around, and a few moments of deduction might have told him which ones to follow—but one look into the back of the patrol car at Cally told him that she needed him the most.

Part of him almost wished she'd never come to British Columbia, too. Not because he regretted her as an assignment, but because she clearly already had enough tragedy to deal with—enough bother from her family and the other people in her life—and adding this trauma to what was supposed be a special season of celebration was clearly only making things worse.

And for some reason, his dumb brain had tried to make it better by kissing her forehead as if they belonged to each other. The gesture had been presumptuous and overly familiar, and he'd been relieved she hadn't been angry.

However, his rebellious emotions wished that he'd been able to kiss her somewhere else instead—with permission first—but that would be even less appropriate under the circumstances. And she'd not given any indication of wanting that, so it was unhealthy to allow the desire to take up any more mental space.

"I'm so sorry," he said again, this time in reference to everything that had happened. "I know I can't make it better, and it must be horrible to be going through this with someone who's essentially a complete stranger. Is there someone I can call? A family member who you do get along with who can just…talk with you for a little while? Maybe we can try a Skype call if the internet is stable enough."

Cally sniffed and wiped her nose with a tissue from her pocket. "Honestly, I just want this to stop. I can't go home, not after what I said to my mother and my family—I don't want to give them a reason to continue bothering me—but I also clearly can't stay here on my own. Nowhere is safe, not the rental cabin, the spa, the church…"

Aaron shared the same concern. Under different circumstances, he'd take her out of Fort Mason and bring her to another town or put her up someplace with a stronger, better-equipped police station, or even just take her to stay with Ellen and her brother. The more people in a house, the less likely a thief was to break in—and it helped that Ellen's brother, Jamie, was also an RCMP officer and could watch her, while having someone else cover his shift. In Fort Mason, that simply wasn't an option.

"I'm going to recommend we go back to the police station," he said. "And I hate to say it, but I think you should probably spend the night there. One of the three of us will be on duty at all times, and I'll open up the back rooms so that you can use the shower and changing area for pajamas, brushing teeth, whatever. I'll grab blankets and pillows."

He slid into the driver's seat and drove them slowly back to the RCMP station. While he had faith that he could get the generator running again to make the place functional for an overnight stay, it was far from ideal. Aaron couldn't help feeling guilty for not being able to offer more.

When he unlocked a side room with a cot, Cally shattered again. She dropped onto the end and buried her face in her hands.

"Hey," he said, sitting next to her. "I'm going to be here until Leo comes to relieve me. I'll be at the front keeping watch. No one will get inside this station to harm you. Do you understand? Not a single person enters this building without RCMP permission. So please, get some rest. Use the facilities as you want, and don't feel bad about asking for a single thing."

She nodded but didn't meet his eyes as he stood and moved to the doorway. Just before Aaron stepped out of the room, Cally spoke, her voice so soft and quiet that he almost didn't hear it.

"Aaron?"

He froze, uncertain if he'd imagined it, but when he glanced over his shoulder, she was staring at him. "Yes?"

Cally sighed and interlaced her fingers in her lap. "Sorry if this seems odd, but you said anything, so… will you sit with me for a little while? Just sit with me?"

His insides, which had turned to black ice after realizing that the 911 calls had been fraudulent, began to melt.

He moved to the edge of the cot and sat down next to her, taking her hand and this time interlacing his fingers with hers instead. "Of course I will."

She rested her head on his shoulder and sighed.

He prayed that the morning would bring some clarity and peace. For both of them.

TEN

Aaron found Cally in the RCMP station break room the next morning. Her complexion was pale, and the puffiness under her eyes told him that she'd spent most of the night crying. He'd been true to his word and kept watch until Leo arrived to relieve him for a few hours of rest, though he and his brother had talked for a while about what had happened with the fake 911 calls and how they were going to handle it.

But truthfully, that was the crux of the problem. They weren't equipped to handle it, and until the roads were unblocked and they could get some backup assistance from Fort St. Jacob, tracing the source of the calls was nearly impossible. And while Cally might have implied last night that she wanted to just give up and go home, Aaron wasn't certain that was a wise move, either. The individual or gang involved continued to be one step ahead, always knowing where Cally would be. She was being watched, and that would make getting her to the airport, on a plane and through the entire process to get back to Amar that much more difficult to safely manage.

Not to mention that having handguns in the mix

added an extra level of complexity that the Fort Mason detachment was totally unprepared to deal with. In Canada, handguns were illegal, almost impossible to obtain and required several permits if the owner wanted to move their gun from one place to another—and even those took ages to acquire and had strict regulations. For Cally's attacker to have a handgun meant the weapon was illegally obtained, adding another tally mark to the incidents in northern British Columbia using these weapons. A shooting earlier in the year had resulted in the arrest of a number of individuals using illegal weapons, but the intel they'd given up on their suppliers had led to several dead ends. The last he'd heard, Ellen's RCMP officer brother, Jamie, was taking over the investigation, but it was slow going.

Which left the matter of how Aaron was going to handle the issue with Cally, and he still wasn't entirely certain what to do next. Especially after what he'd learned while doing a sweep of the precinct last night after Cally had fallen asleep.

"Did you sleep all right?" Aaron sat across from her, but she didn't look up. He knew it was a terrible question the moment he'd said it—it was clear that she hadn't slept well, and he wasn't helping the matter. "Is there anything I can get for you? Name it, and I'll do my best."

She didn't respond for several minutes, but when she finally looked up, he flinched at the hard look in her eyes. He hoped it wasn't directed at him.

"Anything?" Her voice was flat but strong, and a nerve flared in his gut. What was she going to ask him for?

But he still nodded and tapped his fingers on the

table. "Anything that I have the power or ability to get or do. Legally, of course."

Cally sighed and dropped her gaze again. "This might sound crazy, and I know last night I said I couldn't do it, even after saying I wanted to, but I've changed my mind and I think I should go home."

There it was. "I thought you might say that. But I'm not so sure that's a good idea."

She raised her hands, palms up, and lifted her face to the ceiling. "Then I don't know what else to do, Aaron. I'm not safe here, and I'm putting you and everyone else in this town in danger at every turn. Everywhere we go, someone is after me, and it's only getting worse. Someone could have been seriously hurt at the spa, or in town, or what if somebody had been strolling by when I was being shot at inside the car? We don't know what this person or people are capable of. Just because they haven't killed me yet doesn't mean they won't harm others to get to me."

Her voice grew higher in pitch and she spoke faster with each phrase, becoming frantic. "I know you're doing everything you can, but...I can't do this. I just can't. And I know I'll be safe back at home with my extended family. There'll be a million people around watching my every move—no stranger will be able to get within feet of me without someone noticing."

The pain in her voice made Aaron's heart hurt. "And if it's not a stranger?"

She blinked at him. "What?"

"That's the thing. I'm not ruling any angle out at this point. I'm at a total loss." Aaron held a palm out toward her. "Cally." He moved to the seat next to her and placed his hand on her shoulder. "I'm not going to dictate your choices, but let's think this through. Who would take you back to Amar? You can't go on your own, not while there's an armed criminal after you. Regardless of whether it's one person or two, at least one monster has made a point of showing that he can find and get to you almost anywhere. We haven't figured out how he's doing that yet, which means I can't in good conscience send you to Vancouver alone."

"I'm a foreign dignitary, right? Someone can escort me. You can come. Make sure I get on the plane for home, and I'll have my family arrange to be there on the other end. Maybe the embassy here can even contact law enforcement at home and have an escort waiting for me there or tighten security."

"You'd trust your family to be there for you? After all you've told me about them?"

She flinched, lowering her eyes, then grew silent.

He wished he knew the right thing to say to make her feel better, to lessen the fear and pain that had built overnight and was now consuming her. "Cally, I'm not sending you on an international flight right now while your life is in danger. There might be something to the suggestion of involving your embassy, but the risk of letting you go, even taking you myself, is too high. This attacker is brazen and smart." He sighed, took a deep breath and continued. "Someone tried to break into the station last night. While we were responding to the 911 calls. I believe the fake calls were an attempt to separate you from law enforcement, with the intention of breaking in and getting to you while the power and security system was down and no police were around. The person must have quickly realized you weren't there and tracked us down at one of the call locations."

Her face fell, but within the sadness was resignation. "But, the power outage—"

"It was tampered with. We have the generator back online, but a team from BC Hydro has to come in today to fix the lines. They should be heading in anytime now."

Cally's eyes widened and her jaw tensed before she shook her head emphatically. "I'm so stupid. Everything I do is one bad idea after another." She rested her elbows on the table and dropped her chin into her hands. "I can't go anywhere, and I can't stay here and continue to put everyone in this town in danger."

Aaron felt a surge of determination at her words. "You're not stupid. Far from it, in fact. We're both flailing for ideas right now, and mulling over every option is necessary, no matter how far-fetched the ideas might end up being. This isn't your fault, all right? Lord willing, we can wrap all of this up within a few days—before tomorrow night, I hope, because I think you would love the annual Christmas tree lighting in the center of town. I realize that might sound strange, but in spite of all that's happened, you're still a visitor here and it's still my job to try to help you experience what the town has to offer. It's been interrupted so far, but I haven't forgotten why you came here, what you said you'd like to enjoy and experience during the holidays in Canada. We're not going to cancel the tree lighting, but as of right now I can't allow you to attend. It's far too dangerous."

"You think I'd be fired on or attacked in a crowd?"

He shrugged. "I doubt it. And in fact, RCMP protocol is to just beef up security and stay alert. But if it was happening today, I'd tell you to stay here.

Hopefully by the time it rolls around, though, we'll have this all taken care of and you can have a relaxing Christmas."

"I...thank you." Her features softened and she dropped her clasped hands onto the tabletop. "I appreciate hearing that. Maybe it's not realistic to want this solved in time to enjoy a bit of Christmas, but I'm grateful for the thought."

The tiny smile she gave him could have fueled him for a week. How was this woman having such an effect on him? *She's just an assignment. Stay focused on the endgame.*

Which, of course, was the promotion. But somehow the shine of it had dulled.

A promotion would be nice, he admitted to himself, *but it means nothing if I can't protect the people I care about...and, uh, those I'm under orders to protect.*

"In the meantime," he said, "I'll try to figure out a discreet, secure location today where you can stay that isn't a police station. Does that sound good?"

She nodded, but looked uncertain about Aaron's suggestion. Truth be told, Aaron wasn't sure about his plan, either. Could he solve this in twenty-four hours? It was probably a long shot, but he'd try. And once Cally had a safe place to lay her head, he'd be able to think more clearly and perhaps even find a way to target the criminal. He had no idea how he'd draw the attacker out into the open without endangering Cally, but as much as he wanted to catch the perp and end this, if it came to choosing between keeping Cally safe and arresting the criminal, he knew which one he'd pick every time.

It's my imperative to keep her safe as much as it is

to bring criminals to justice, he rationalized. *Nothing emotion-driven about that.*

He'd always been a terrible liar.

Cally watched Aaron in her peripheral vision as she scrolled through the messages on her phone, reams of delayed texts and email notifications that she still hadn't caught up on since cell service had returned the day prior. Her stomach squeezed with hope as she searched for some indication that Aaron had been right—that all her relatives wanted was for her to be safe and happy—but the squeezing shifted to a stabbing emptiness as she swiped to delete each and every one, until she came to a text from her uncle.

"Uh, Aaron?"

He glanced up from his paperwork, pen clamped between his lips. Cally almost smiled. He looked cute, vulnerable. He raised one eyebrow at her, and for a moment, her fear and anxiety melted away. And then his gaze flicked to her phone, and it all came rushing back.

"My uncle texted," she said, turning the screen so Aaron could see. She'd hit the translate option so he could read it in English. "He's boarding a plane soon to come up here. He spoke to my mother last night. She called him in a panic after speaking with me."

Aaron took the pen out of his mouth. "He was already in Vancouver?"

"He is now. Until last night he was in Ottawa, for a conference. But he works for the Department of Natural Resources in Amar. He was about to fly home. There's usually a plane change and a bit of a layover before going the rest of the way back. Nobody offers direct flights."

Aaron sighed. "Can you tell him not to come? I don't think it's wise to bring someone else into this situation. Another family member might complicate things."

Cally fired off a reply to her uncle and waited. "I agree. I was just going to call him and say Merry Christmas, not try to con him into joining me here. Of course my mother had to overreact and call him. She probably begged and guilted him into flying up to check on me in person. Why can't she just…" Cally dropped her head to the tabletop, forehead pressed against her splayed fingers.

Her phone buzzed, and she nudged it toward Aaron without looking at it first.

"He's boarding," Aaron said a moment later. She didn't miss the undercurrent of frustration in his voice, too.

Cally peered up at him, not at all surprised to see the tension increasing in his neck and jaw. "I'm sorry. This means someone is going to have to pick him up from the airport, too, doesn't it?"

"Yes. And before you ask, no, you're not going. I'll send Leo. I'm not comfortable taking you on that journey. But there's another problem we'll have to deal with first."

What now? She groaned and laid her head back down on the table. In the darkness behind her eyes, memories began to replay on a stuck loop.

The patrol car slamming into the ditch. The attacker in the grocery store coming closer as she ran out of places to hide. Feeling like a caged animal as she stared down the barrel of a gun through the car window.

She gripped her stomach with both hands, struck by a wave of nausea.

"Cally?" Aaron's chair scraped backward as he jumped to his feet. "What is it—oh, your stomach? Hang on. I have a ginger chew around here that's good for settling an upset stomach." He rummaged in a desk for a minute, then handed her a candy. She took it and ate it as he talked. He settled into the seat next to her once again and ran his hand across her back while the ginger did its work.

He continued, "I was going to say—" and Cally was grateful for the distraction "—that my parents might be willing to house you and your uncle. You can't stay here overnight a second time. We're still on generator power and it's going to run out any moment. We'll only have until daylight fades, unless power gets up and running again before then."

"Is that a possibility? Can the repair trucks or whoever get to us by then?"

"Yes, I just got an update that they're already on the way. The roads are supposed to be fine today," he said. "They're probably almost cleared by now, actually. And from the sounds of things, the tail end of the storm moved out last night, so we're in the clear for at least a few days. It'll be cold, though. The temperature will drop, so none of the snow we have right now will melt. That said, don't get too comfortable—there'll be another wave of snow soon enough. There always is. Maybe not so much, though."

Cally's response was a groan. It was all she could muster at the thought of more snow.

"I was thinking, though, that even if we move you, we make it seem like you're still here. The culprit clearly knows when you come and go through the front door, but two can play at that game. I've got a plan—

my mom can bring over a large tote bag or large purse, something inconspicuous, and load anything you need into it. A change of clothes, that type of thing. I'll have my parents drive their car around to the rear doors of the station to load you and leave, so you can slip out the back and hunker down in the back seat. My parents' home also has a garage entrance. I doubt our criminal friends are going to be watching the back door of the police station, since they'd have to be on our property to do so, and we have security for that. And there's no way they can see inside a closed garage."

"Really? If your parents are willing, that would be very generous of them." She felt a twinge of relief at the thought of sleeping in a proper bed tonight, and her stomach had calmed slightly thanks to the ginger. She'd almost started to feel normal again. *Almost.* "Do your parents know what's going on? I don't want to put them at risk."

"To a degree, yes, I've let them in on what's happening. Don't worry about them. They have a pull-out couch in the basement and an air mattress, and my dad is a former RCMP officer. He's got heavy home security because that's just the way he operates—including a well-trained but super sweet German shepherd named Starbuck—and in a pinch he can still take a bad guy down. He might hurt his back while doing it, but he'll do it." Aaron smiled, and Cally was surprised to find that the sight made her smile, too.

The moment stretched between them, the pressure of his hand on her back a strong and welcome comfort. Was she mistaken, or had his hand lingered overlong? Cally couldn't help but think that something very important was happening—and she didn't want the moment to end.

A knock came on the front doors, and Cally yelped in surprise.

"Who...? Are you expecting someone?"

Aaron reached up and squeezed her shoulder. "No, but it could be anyone. I'll go check. I locked the doors for safety, but technically this is still a working police station. If a citizen needs help, all they have to do is knock or ring the doorbell. Hold tight."

Cally released the breath that had caught in her chest. Of course. For one brief moment, she'd forgotten that Aaron was an on-duty RCMP officer. He fit so well into the quiet spaces, into conversation, that it was easy to forget he was working and not simply spending time with her while she visited.

Cally tried not to eavesdrop, but sound carried in the small building. She heard the doors open, and an unmistakably feminine voice drifted toward the break room. The woman sounded young and eager, not at all like a frightened or upset resident searching for police help. Aaron's tone didn't match, but the woman's volume rose...and moments later, footsteps clacked down the hall toward the break room.

"No!" Aaron shouted. "No, you can't go back there—"

Cally tensed with alarm. Should she hide? Find something to defend herself with? She popped out of her chair and picked it up, flipping it around as she sidestepped toward the doorway—and then a familiar blonde entered the room, wearing a puffy white winter coat and holding a large cellophane-wrapped gift basket in her arms.

"Tricia?" Cally stared at the spa owner and then searched for Aaron, who hurried down toward the break room with obvious frustration. She lowered the chair, feeling foolish for her overreaction.

"Tricia has something for you," Aaron said. His words were flat and clipped. "The roads from the spa are apparently more or less safe to drive on, so she came down. However, that also means I need to call the other guys and make a plan to get the patrol car back here. You'll be all right for a few minutes?"

"Of course we will, silly," Tricia said. She plunked the gift basket on the table and patted Aaron's arm, letting her hand linger on his biceps. Aaron cleared his throat and took a step backward. Tricia's smile wavered as she glanced from Aaron to Cally and back again. Then, her smile a little wider but too taut to be genuine, she slid into a seat at the table and rolled her eyes at Cally. "He worries about the oddest things, doesn't he?"

"I wouldn't say it's odd to be concerned after several attempts have been made on Cally's life," Aaron replied. Cally locked eyes with him and offered a shallow nod. She'd be fine with Tricia for a few minutes. The woman was harmless, if a little lovestruck.

As Aaron hurried away, Tricia turned her attention on Cally. Her smile was still bright and friendly, but something about it seemed...off. The expression didn't quite reach her eyes, tautness shifting into an almost forced desperation. Cally felt bad for her—Tricia seemed otherwise nice, and Cally admired the woman's business acumen that had allowed her to develop a successful, prestigious local business.

"Tricia, you didn't have to come here and bring... this." Cally waved at the massive wicker basket the spa owner had placed in the middle of the table. It was filled with an assortment of soaps, lotions and chocolates.

"Don't be ridiculous," Tricia said. "Bringing by a personal apology is the least I can do. Mind you, I assumed I'd simply drop it off here and have the boys deliver it for me, but here you are! I can't apologize enough for what happened yesterday. I'm still shaken, so I can't even imagine how you're feeling."

"I appreciate your concern. I'm feeling better today, thank you. Aaron—uh, Officer Thrace has done an excellent job of making me feel comfortable and easing my anxiety about the situation. I'm not going to pretend I'm not afraid, but he's helping."

Tricia raised an eyebrow and her smile tightened further. "Is he, now? That's very kind of him. He's a good man. Very handsome, too."

Cally didn't disagree, but she couldn't help sensing that she was being baited. "Very kind" was all she decided to respond with.

Tricia pursed her lips, then pulled her fingers through her hair. "You know, he and I used to be quite the item around town. Some years ago."

It *was* bait, then. What did Tricia want? Some kind of validation? Cally was beginning to get the sense that Aaron had understated the degree to which Tricia was still emotionally attached to him. The way her eyes narrowed as she spoke suggested that Tricia felt she continued to hold a claim on him.

The best response Cally could muster was a polite smile, after which she turned her attentions on the gift basket. "Lavender Epsom salts, how lovely! This is such a generous gift. I really appreciate it, and I'll be sure to share it with Ellen and let her know you went out of your way to bring this over. She spoke so highly of your spa that I have no doubt she'll want to reschedule, so you won't lose the business."

Tricia looked over her shoulder, back down the hall where Aaron had vanished. They could hear him on the phone, voice low and no-nonsense. When Tricia turned back to face Cally, she leaned in as if they were good friends about to have a casual chat. "You're so sweet, you and Ellen. Ellen is marrying Aaron's brother— I assume you knew that already. All of the Thrace brothers are quite the catch, but this latest wedding must be making Aaron eager to get hitched himself, now that he'll be the last Thrace standing, so to speak. Being the eldest and unmarried, I wonder if he feels any pressure… One must be careful, I imagine, in case his desperation causes him to throw himself at any old woman in his path. Even if she's not the right one for him, you know?"

Yes, Tricia was definitely baiting her and trying to dig for information. "He's not a teenager," Cally said. She leaned back in her chair and folded her arms. "And I'm not into gossip. If you're concerned, I'd recommend that you speak to him personally."

Tricia tapped the table with her long nails. "You know what? I will, when he has a moment. Speaking of, how long will you be in town?"

"Until after the wedding," Cally said, though Tricia would know she'd be around at least that long.

"Flying home for Christmas Day?"

"No, after. It's too expensive to charter a plane a few days before Christmas." Among other reasons, but that was another conversation entirely, and not one she knew Tricia well enough to engage in.

"I also hear you're not at the cabin on the west side of town anymore, so where are you staying?" She leaned in farther, her smile still pasted on and a little unnerving. "If you'd like, I can come there and finish some of your treatments like the pedicure—"

How was she supposed to respond to that? "I…"

"I'm sure Cally will be happy to return to the spa as soon as your security cameras are up and running properly, and I give the all clear," Aaron said as he walked into the room. Tricia's face lit up with genuine excitement as he approached her, but fell in confusion as he tossed the USB key she'd given him onto the table. "Though that may be longer than anticipated. There was nothing on the footage. By which I mean the footage was blank. My trust in your ability to handle security of any kind has been greatly diminished."

Tricia's lips parted but she said nothing. Cally wasn't sure if this news came as a surprise, or if the woman was trying to come up with an explanation.

Aaron didn't wait for either. "But you knew that already, didn't you."

"Aaron—" Tricia began.

"Tricia, you can't do this. You can't hand an RCMP officer a fake security clip and then barge into the situation to apologize—you realize how that makes you look, right? I could arrest you for potential obstruction by giving me this nonexistent footage just to make yourself look good and your business look compliant, not to mention your act of trespassing by running down here to the staff room after being directly told not to by a *federal officer.*"

Tricia frowned and stood. "I didn't know it was blank. I promise. I moved over the digital files from backup, dated with yesterday's date and time stamp of when the incident occurred. Maybe the flickering power messed up the cameras, or—"

"Or you wanted a reason to come down here." Aaron crossed his arms and sighed. "Did you bring a second flash drive with the real footage?"

Cally's stomach churned again as Tricia shook her head. Despite Aaron's words, Tricia moved closer to his side, as if drawn to him by compulsion. Cally felt sorry for her; she clearly had unresolved feelings for Aaron, but was expressing them in a very unhealthy way. Not to mention that her questions about Cally's whereabouts had been a little too pointed. Like she was trying to gather information.

Like she came here to dig for intel and brought the gift basket in an effort to gain my trust to get it.

And although the person who'd attacked Cally at the spa had definitely been a man, Aaron had mentioned his suspicion that the attacker from the rental cabin hadn't been acting alone.

That made almost anyone a suspect. Especially the bright-eyed woman standing across from her…who was also wearing a white winter coat. *Like one of the attackers.*

Tricia must have felt Cally's eyes on her, because her head slowly turned to meet Cally's stare. Her expression darkened.

And then her hand moved to the side of her waistband, as if deliberately reaching for something holstered inside.

ELEVEN

"Hey! Freeze!" Aaron's voice boomed through the staff room. "Hands where I can see them." He whipped around to stand between Tricia and Cally, facing the woman who'd come to visit. Tricia gasped and, seeing his hands on his Taser, backed away.

"What did I do?" She lifted her hands up. "I'm trying to take a card out of my pocket."

He wasn't about to relax until he was certain she was telling the truth. "Slowly. Make sure I can see your hands at all times."

Tricia reached into her pocket and pulled out a small, laminated card. She held it up, fingers shaking, expression growing more furious by the second. "I was going to hand this to Cally. It has my personal cell phone number on it. I only give these to my clients who pay a premium for home visits. If she and Ellen want to get their pre-wedding treatments done, I'm willing to come to them at the same discounted rate I was going to offer for coming to the spa."

He took the card and handed it back to Tricia. "Why were you asking about her accommodations?"

"So I could figure out the timing between clients at the spa and traveling to wherever she's staying."

"Nice coat. Had it long?"

"It *is* nice, thank you. It's none of your business, but I bought it on clearance last week in Fort St. Jacob. What's your problem, Thrace? You weren't this trigger-happy when we were together."

Aaron resisted the urge to growl at Tricia in frustration. "That was a long time ago. The past is the past, and right now I'm doing my job. The same way you're evidently trying to do yours. If you don't mind, I'd appreciate it if you left now. I'll be sending Hatch by your workplace soon to check into the security footage. I hope he discovers that you're telling the truth and that there truly hasn't been any sort of tampering. Or that you lied to a federal officer about having security cameras operating in the first place."

Tricia instantly looked crestfallen, but Aaron wasn't about to be fooled. He saw the hard calculation in her eyes, and while he didn't think she'd lied intentionally—that wasn't like her—he also couldn't dismiss her actions. Regardless of Tricia's claims of innocence, Cally's life was on the line, and he wasn't going to let anyone get away with foolish behavior that might compromise the integrity of an RCMP investigation.

She took a step toward him, hand reaching for his arm, but he stepped back before she made contact. Another idea sprang to mind, but he had a suspicion she wasn't going to like it. "Tricia, will you submit to questioning regarding your whereabouts these past few days?"

Tricia blinked up at him—fierce and defiant—but then her gaze flicked behind him to where Cally stood, and she nodded instead. "Of course. You're just doing your job. Happy to cooperate."

"Great," Aaron said. "If you have a few minutes right now, I'll show you to an interview room. Officer Hatch will be over shortly to take your statement, then he can follow you back to the spa to check on that security situation."

Tricia's jaw dropped as she tried to protest, but Aaron wasn't having any of it. He led her to a room and closed the door, then called Hatch to ask him to come and do the interview. He'd get nowhere trying to speak to her himself—the woman clearly had ulterior motives in mind when she'd come to the police station. Aaron waited for Hatch to arrive, briefed his fellow officer, then returned to the break room.

Cally lay on the staff room futon, curled into herself. Her body was tense, shoulders hunched as one arm cradled her head. Her other arm was pulled in tight to her chest. He stood in the doorway for a moment, not wanting to disturb her in case she'd fallen asleep. He'd been awake most of the night again, taking turns on shift with Hatch and Leo, and he'd heard her tossing and turning on the small cot they'd set up for her. After all she'd been through, she deserved some peace—but he had a feeling it'd be a while before she got it.

The very fact that she hadn't yelled at him or tried to run off and solve things on her own, however, made him want to try that much harder to make things right. She obviously didn't see herself as a patient person, but he was impressed by how she continued to take the hits in stride—she allowed herself to be upset, and then moved on. Practical. Focused.

Experienced in dealing with trauma.

The thought pained his heart. If he'd lost someone he loved as suddenly as she had, and if his family then started pestering him the way hers was doing, he didn't think he'd be handling it with the same grace.

He'd never been all that patient *or* gracious, though his professional life didn't necessarily show it. It had taken years of schooling and training before he'd become a full-fledged RCMP officer, and having the honor of performing in the Mounted Ride in Ottawa had been an incredible experience, and worth all the time and effort. But outside of his career, patience wasn't a virtue he held on to very well. When he was younger, he and his youngest brother, Sam, had fought more than they'd gotten along, usually due to Sam's obstinate behavior and Aaron's lack of patience for his antics. They'd gotten into many physical altercations, and Aaron had once even broken his brother's nose.

Out of the three Thrace brothers, Aaron had been the only one who'd known pretty much since birth what he'd wanted to do with his life: follow in his father's footsteps and join the RCMP. It had been a blessing that his brother Leo had decided to do the same, but Sam had only joined after a life-changing experience, finally changing his *laissez-faire* ways when the love of his life had broken his heart. Ever since Sam's transformation, he and Aaron had gotten along much better, but Aaron still had to work hard at being patient with others and not allowing his perfectionist tendencies to get the better of him. As the oldest child, it was hard not to feel like he knew better all the time.

Even his parents' questions—though infrequent—about his love life raised his hackles, because he was just as impatient as they were. On the other hand, he hardly had time to attend to all of his duties in Fort Mason, let alone consider adding in a wife and maybe a future family of his own. And if the RCMP moved him to another province or another detachment within British Columbia, well, he'd have plenty more to deal with.

Why am I even thinking about a wife and family, Lord? He hadn't allowed himself that indulgence for a very long time. But spending the past few days with Cally had forced him to admit that a capable, personality-compatible partner in life and in love really was the absolute, exact thing he'd always wanted.

In fact, someone like *her* was the exact thing he'd always wanted.

Too bad she belonged to another country, another place. She had responsibilities of her own, and had experienced nothing but disruption and pain since arriving in Fort Mason.

He gently cleared his throat and she roused, blinked up at him and smiled.

His insides melted and his patience with himself waned. He'd only known this woman for less than two days, and yet already he was trying to hide the truth from himself.

Whether he liked it or not, he was falling in love.

Cally's anxiety skyrocketed with each passing hour. While Aaron seemed perfectly capable at completing his paperwork and conducting the investigation from behind a desk—a necessary part of the job, she was well aware, plus the wisest course of action while trying to keep her safe—she couldn't relax. Despite his insistence that they were safe inside the police station, instead of feeling protected, she just felt restless and trapped.

Did she trust Tricia's assertion that her interest in

Cally's visit was purely business-related? That it didn't actually have to do with what she thought she might have witnessed after the attack at the spa? Unrequited love sometimes made people react in extremes, and Aaron had implied that this wasn't the first time Tricia had acted strangely under the guise of trying to get close to him—or get back together with him. Did Tricia really see Cally as a threat? Had she been trying to scare Cally off, resorting to outrageous measures and using weapons after seeing Aaron's and Cally's faces a little too close together when they'd been sitting next to each other in the hallway? Tricia had asked a lot of questions, but she didn't seem like the type of person to attack and shoot at somebody. Plus, the attacks had started the day prior to that incident.

Then again, weren't most criminals also great actors? And Tricia had taken an obscenely long time to respond to the call button after Cally had pressed it. It was almost as if Tricia had been purposefully killing time—giving someone else a chance to get to the room first. The room had also had a convenient escape route, though it had required breaking a window. As outlandish as the suspicion seemed, Tricia's visit still wasn't sitting right.

"How are you feeling?" Aaron entered the room, wearing more gear than he'd sported earlier. Was he planning to go somewhere?

She shrugged and rubbed her temples. "I've been better, but that's no surprise. I've been trying to rack my brain over why this might be happening, but it seems like your abduction for ransom theory is the best one we have so far. Unless you have a new lead and a different idea?"

"Yes and no. The interview with Tricia didn't reveal any more pertinent details. I know, pretty much everyone is a suspect right now, but I still have reservations about her guilt."

Cally nodded, wanting to trust him. He seemed like the kind of man who saw the good side of everyone—even if his job probably wanted him to do the opposite—and she appreciated that. "Maybe she's just a woman in love who doesn't know how to handle it?"

Aaron's cheeks turned pink. "Uh, well…"

"It's nothing to be ashamed of. She's not your responsibility. I think she's otherwise a nice person. I only wish our conversation had been about more substantial topics—she *is* a successful business owner, after all. I could learn a few things from her about client relationships that might help with my freelance contracts."

He leaned against the doorframe and crossed his arms. "Are you being serious?"

"I am. Provided she's not behind the attacks, that is." Cally sat upright and gestured to Aaron's outfit. "But what's with the getup?"

Aaron fiddled with his radio for a moment before responding. "The guys found an abandoned snowmobile in a back field and have brought it to the local garage for testing—fingerprints, serial numbers and so forth. Leo also found evidence of a break-in at Mrs. Henderson's home, which tells us that of the three phony 911 calls, at least one was made on-location. Mrs. Henderson likely had no idea—I mean, her hearing has mostly gone anyway, so someone sneaking around might have been able to get in and out without her noticing. The call from the church also probably came from on-location—there was apparently some-one working in the main office at the time that I was wandering around searching for the source of the call, but that individual had stepped out to take a parcel to the post office. The church doesn't lock its doors in general, so it would have been easy to get inside and make a call before slipping away."

"But didn't you say a woman made one of those calls?"

"Yes, a woman made one of the calls, according to the operator I spoke with. The other two calls came from male callers, but honestly, that's not something we can trust, either. There are phone apps that can record your voice and then alter it. I listened to the 911 calls, and it's entirely possible they were prerecorded. People don't use natural cadence when making emergency calls due to the high-adrenaline nature of the moment, so it's hard to tell a true call from a false recording."

"So you don't think there are two people working together? Just one?"

"I honestly don't want to rule it out either way. We could have one person, two or three, and I can't rule out male or female. We know at least one of the individuals involved is male, but that's all we can say for sure. What I do know is that they're not going to be able to continue to get away with this. The entire town has been alerted to the situation, and as soon as we receive a phone call with information on a suspicious person, an unrecognized vehicle or any other unusual activity, we're going to be on it.

"Finding the snowmobile is a huge break. It gives us something to go on, or it will once we search the reg-istration records to help us pinpoint where the vehicle came from—then we can figure out who sold or rented it, and to whom. If it's a rental, the rental place may even have video security footage. And if not, unless it was a cash sale, there's going to be a paper trail, either through credit cards or a rental agreement. As far as I'm aware, there are no shady rental companies around here—and if it's a privately owned off-road vehicle, the province has pretty strict paper trail requirements."

"Unless it's a stolen snowmobile, in which case the owner is probably panicking."

"And if that's the case, we'll deal with it when it comes to that. But you'd think that if someone noticed their snowmobile missing, they'd call us. I mean, where is the thief going to go? All the way to Vancouver? I mean, it sounds elaborate, but we're in a very small town. People notice things. Getting away with medium- to large-scale crime is nearly impossible."

"Except for the illegal guns thing?" She felt bad when Aaron winced. "Sorry. I shouldn't have brought it up."

He sighed, but nodded. "Yes, okay. That's major, and very serious. But Ellen's brother, Jamie, is on the case for it, so it's not within our wheelhouse. If this case brings any leads, great, but otherwise it's not my assignment. I'd be handing off any intel to someone else."

Cally stood, stretching her back and legs. Sitting around the police station was not only driving her stir-crazy, it was also making her body cramp up. "That's fair. I guess you have your hands full enough with these thefts. Do you work multiple cases at a time, though? I suppose you must."

"We do, especially here. The RCMP is a federal police force, but in rural areas like Fort Mason, we serve as the local police. Sometimes we take on more federal-based assignments, though. Special tasks, that sort of thing."

"Like what?" Now she was curious. "If you're federal, does that mean you're like the FBI?"

A tiny smile curved the corner of his mouth. "In some ways. We do deal with some national incidents. We also escort foreign dignitaries, for example."

"Oh, right." She laughed. "Like me, apparently."

"Yeah." He looked back over his shoulder. "I have a few more things to finish up, then my parents will be over to covertly move you to their home, if you're okay with that. Or we can wait until your uncle gets here, but I thought that might be a little more conspicuous than my parents coming and going from the station. Any update from your uncle lately?"

She checked her phone. The last she'd heard from him was about two hours ago, a final text as the cabin was instructed to put their phones in flight mode. "He should be here soon, I'd think. He'll let me know when he arrives, and I'll tell you right away."

"Great. Leo is ready to head out to get him."

She thanked him and tried to plaster on an expression of contentment while he went back to work. But inside, all she felt was churning acid. Staying indoors in the station felt like a constant state of anticipation, waiting for the next terrible thing to happen.

But despite all the terrifying attacks she'd been through in such a short time, she found herself trusting that Aaron would see them through. She hoped, truly and deeply, that he'd be able to find and arrest the attackers as quickly as possible, because as much as she'd come to terms with having Uncle Zarek visit, she didn't relish the thought of bringing anyone else into the line of fire and ruining someone else's holiday.

Secondary to that, however, was the strange and invasive thought that if Uncle Zarek didn't stick around for more than a day or two—and if Aaron was able to catch these attackers as quickly as he hoped to—there was a chance, however slight, that she might spend some stress-free time alone with the handsome RCMP officer.

Just to say thank you, she told herself. *Just to show my appreciation for everything he's done for me.*

But as Aaron walked back into the room to refill his coffee, offering up a genuine half smile as he passed by, Cally knew that wasn't true. As strange as it was, and as guilty as she felt for it, she had feelings for Aaron—and she didn't have a clue what to do about them.

TWELVE

Aaron kept a close watch on the front of the RCMP station. His parents were due to arrive any minute to transfer Cally over to their home, and he felt increasingly uncomfortable at the thought of her leaving his sight. Just because there hadn't been a deliberate attack since yesterday didn't mean the culprit wasn't outside someplace, hiding and waiting...

The upside was that, since returning from the spa, Hatch had been able to park around the corner to keep watch on the building, just in case. The downside was that he couldn't stay there forever, not with the detachment's limited resources. Not to mention that his review of the spa's security system had revealed very little. It was difficult to tell whether it'd been deliberately tampered with, or if the system had gone out due to the power outages. They'd called Fort St. Jacob to ask for a tech expert to come in—and served an official warrant to the spa—but it was going to be a day or two before the expert arrived.

The radio buzzed on his belt—Leo was likely calling from his car, on the way to receive Cally's uncle. Cell service had grown spotty again as the wind outside had picked up, blowing around yesterday's snow and generally making a worse mess of an already dicey weather situation. He felt bad for the town's community volunteer crew who were currently attempting to set up for tomorrow's tree lighting event. They'd have a hard time doing much of anything.

"How's the drive?" Aaron said in response to the radio call. Footsteps came toward him down the hall, and he glanced up to see Cally settling into a chair in the public waiting area. She looked nervous...or was that loneliness?

"Terrible," Leo said. "I'm pulling into the airport now. Looks like the plane is landing. Good thing, too, with how this wind is gusting. I heard back from the garage and sent you a message that the snowmobile was rented at a place on the other side of town, the one down the road from the spa—did you get that?"

"I did. Sorry, I didn't get a chance to follow up with you on that, but I have some ideas. Let me know when you're coming back into town, and I'll make sure Cally is over at Mom and Dad's." Cally glanced up at the sound of her name. Aaron gave her a thumbs-up, which she acknowledged with a tiny half smile. "Drop him off there, too, and then come back to the station," he continued. "I want to head out to the snowmobile rental place and ask the owner a few questions, see if they have any security footage we can check out. They'll have a rental agreement. That's not something the rental place can get around, so it could be the break we're looking for."

"You're going to leave Roslin with Mom and Dad? And her uncle, I guess. But shouldn't you be at the station, or at least nearby in case of emergency? She trusts you. The rental shop is fifteen minutes east in good weather."

Aaron ran his hand down the side of his face. The weather was making this investigation difficult to organize and conduct, and while he was fully aware that couldn't be helped, it didn't mean he felt any better about the lack of progress thus far.

He'd promised to do his best to bring the criminal responsible for the attacks to justice by the end of today, in time for the event tomorrow, but he was hardly closer to a resolution than he'd been on the day of Cally's arrival. She trusted him to get this taken care of, she'd told him so more than once, and yet he continued to fail her at every turn.

Not to mention that there was no way she'd be giving a favorable report on his work after the assignment had ended. He'd never get his promotion.

Though, truth be told, the promotion was the furthest thing from his mind right now. Ever since admitting to himself that he had romantic feelings for her, Cally was all he could think about. Even now, she sat only a few meters away, and yet it felt as if they were miles apart. There was no point in indulging any of his emotions, not when a future with her was an impossibility.

The thought was a harsh reality. He wished he could escape the station for a breath of fresh air, to clear his head.

"Plus," Leo said, voice crackling through the radio static, "we need to find a way to wrap this up, because you'll be needed at the tree lighting tomorrow."

"I'm not sure I can legitimately let Cally attend that." He sighed. "Not with the danger still present."

"You think these goons would make another abduction attempt in a town full of RCMP officers? There'll be at least ten of us, plus volunteers and auxiliary. Someone draws a weapon and they're not making it two feet before we're on them."

That gave Aaron pause. There *were* ten additional officers plus extra help coming into Fort Mason for the tree lighting—an unusual amount for such a small town, but the local detachments cooperated to support each other during holiday events. Besides, nearly every resident who'd remained in town, plus folks in the surrounding area and plenty from Fort St. Jacob, would be driving in for the event. In return, citizens from Fort Mason would drive down to Fort St. Jacob for their Christmas parade next Friday, and everyone from both towns would go to the holiday lights show at Schroeder Lake on Christmas Eve.

There'd be hundreds of people and a significant security presence in Fort Mason's town square. Leo wasn't wrong—anyone who produced a weapon would be taken down immediately. A thief wouldn't get far, either. All factors considered, Cally would be safe as long as she remained in full view of himself and the other officers—in fact, probably safer in a public gathering than if she stayed at the police station, though he'd already drawn up multiple scenario response plans in case one of her attackers became impatient and decided to simply stride through the front door. Not that he thought anyone would get far if they stepped into the police station. They'd be identified and the station locked down in seconds—well, provided they had full power restored first.

But judging by how shaken Cally had been when

ensconced safely inside the patrol car and had a gun drawn on her, he didn't want to imagine what it would be like if someone started rapping on the doors, or shaking door handles, or shooting at the glass to try to get into the station.

"I'm thinking we keep the visitors near you and pull in two of the Fort St. Jacob guys to watch your six in the meantime," Leo suggested. "Okay? I'll brief Biers as soon as I've dropped off the visitor and finished up at the rental shop, then call to update."

Aaron begrudgingly agreed, then hung up and glanced over the desk to check on Cally—and found her watching him, a stricken expression on her face. He hurried over to her. She had her phone in her hands, tapping the device against her palm over and over.

"Is everything all right? What's wrong?"

Cally blinked as though trying to process whatever information she'd received. "I just spoke to Ellen. I guess Tricia called to update her on the offer to do a private booking, the same thing she suggested to me during her visit here. Anyway, Ellen thought it sounded great and rescheduled a few treatments for the two of us. At your parents' place."

"And?"

"The spa just called her to cancel."

Aaron shrugged. "That's not so unusual. The next day or so will be pretty busy for the town, since the tree lighting is tomorrow. All those empty streets will have plenty of people, residents and visitors, so everyone is preparing."

"No, that's not the important part." Cally stared at him, her eyes wide with concern and a hint of fear. "They canceled because Tricia didn't show up for her afternoon clients. And she's not answering her calls. No one can get in touch with her. Aaron, Tricia has gone MIA. And she knows where I'm staying tonight."

Cally's heart pounded in her chest as Aaron growled under his breath and got back on the phone. She listened as he made calls to the spa, to the other officers and to Ellen to find out exactly what she'd said to Tricia. She also heard him on the phone with someone who she suspected was his father.

She tried deep breathing through waves of lightheadedness. She didn't want to believe the spa owner had anything to do with the attacks, but…it was too strange that she'd up and disappeared. When Aaron marched back down the hallway to the staff room, the intensity on his face only aggravated her anxiety. "Did you learn anything?" she asked, hopeful.

Aaron shook his head. "No. Her cousin—who lives here in Fort Mason—seems to think that Tricia might have driven south to visit her boyfriend for the holidays, based on a cryptic text message she received a few hours ago. But everyone else associated with her doesn't even recall her mentioning a boyfriend, and it's odd that she'd skip out on clients the day before the tree lighting, when the spa is charging a premium for their services. And without telling anybody. That's as far as we've gotten with it, but the boyfriend angle is something the Fort St. Jacob team can help us work on with social media."

Boyfriend! The woman certainly hadn't acted as though she was attached to anyone, especially not with the probing questions about Aaron and the way she'd kept trying to move closer to him, to touch his arms, shoulders, anywhere she could reach.

"Aaron, I honestly doubt she has a boyfriend." Cally sighed and plunged ahead, unsure how he'd react to her suspicions. "Not based on how I've watched her act around you." Her jaw tightened.

"I think you're right," Aaron said. "I know we men can be clueless sometimes, but Tricia hasn't exactly been subtle about her continued affections. I have a hard time believing she has anything to do with these attacks against you, though…"

His eyes grew unfocused as he retreated inward.

"What is it?" Cally prodded. She reached out to touch his arm, but pulled away when she realized what she was doing. Why had she done that? Since when was *she* the one to reach out physically to another person? She was still trying to figure out what had gotten into her last night when she'd asked him to sit with her. He'd given her a lengthy side hug, providing the comfort she'd needed after an emotionally and physically exhausting day.

It had been a long time since she'd felt comfortable enough around someone else to be close to them by choice.

She kept her voice even and low to ask her next question. "Has Tricia done anything like this before?"

"Actually, yes." Aaron folded his arms across his chest with a heavy exhale. "A few years ago, I attended a church barbecue where I met someone. This person had recently moved to the area to take a job at the spa—an aesthetician position. We went out for coffee and had a really nice time…and a few days later, I learned that she'd been fired from the new job. I don't recall the reason Tricia gave for letting her go, but it was pretty ridiculous. I mean, it's not easy to entice people to take jobs up here—Fort Mason is literally in the middle of nowhere—so to fire a perfectly capable employee out of jealousy… It takes a special kind of delusion to do that. But firing someone and firing *at* someone are two completely separate issues."

Cally had to agree. "As awful as that is, and while it can't be denied that people in love will sometimes go to extremes to get what they want, I don't want to think the worst of her—I don't know her that well." She clasped her hands in front of her lips, trying to give shape to an idea bouncing around inside her head. "Aaron, what if she *didn't* run off or go into hiding because she thinks the RCMP are on to her? You said yourself, these culprits seem to know my every move and are likely watching the police station somehow. The break-in they tried yesterday didn't go as planned. What if…what if the people after me saw her leaving the station, followed her and nabbed *her* for information?"

Aaron's eyes widened for a split second before his shoulders drooped. "And the boyfriend story, it could be a coded message, a cry for help, since I'd see the lie immediately." He pulled the radio off his belt. "That's a very astute theory, and one we can't rule out. Though I don't know why she wouldn't have sent the message directly to me, if that was the case. Or maybe she thought I'd ignore it or delete it. I wasn't exactly patient with her while she was here, but I'll speak to Hatch and ask if he saw anything unusual when he was with her."

That didn't solve the main problem, however, and Cally was feeling increasingly sick to her stomach.

They'd finally figured out one last safe place for her to stay in town, and now she didn't even have that. It wasn't Ellen's fault for telling Tricia—she hadn't known the details of what was happening—but it complicated matters further.

"Does this mean I'm going to have to spend another night in the police station? And my uncle, as well?"

Aaron grimaced. "As much as I want to say no, I think I'd better call my parents and let them know not to—"

The station lights flickered and died. The hum of the station's backup generator went silent, and the warm air that had been directed into the room through the heat register overhead stopped blowing. Cally's heart sank even further.

"Great. Does that mean the power is gone for good?"

Aaron groaned and covered his face with one hand. "Why, Lord?" he muttered, before responding to Cally. "Yes, it does. The BC Hydro repair crew is here now, working to restore power to the grid—it needs to be up and running for the tree lighting, obviously—but since the station is at the edge of town, we're usually one of the last places on the grid to come back online."

Cally sidled up to a window to check outside. As it had in the days since her arrival, daylight was fading fast. "How long, do you think?"

"No way to know," Aaron said. "Could be an hour, could be six hours. We don't have another generator to run, which means…well, it means emergency protocol. Our RCMP base of operations needs to move elsewhere, so I'm going to have to commandeer either the community hall or another building with power, and take some of our computers and radios over there.

I'll have to lock down this building, which means you can't stay here."

Cally's throat tightened. *Please, Lord. I know we haven't talked much and You probably don't even want to hear from me, but please. Extend some grace.*

"Does this mean I'm going to your parents' place after all?"

Aaron nodded as a knock sounded on the back door. "I guess it does. Let's pray we can pull this transfer off without the wrong people noticing."

She zipped up her winter coat and slid on her gloves, trying not to think about what might happen if this plan went sideways. "Way ahead of you."

THIRTEEN

Aaron opened the back door to let his father inside. His parents' car was pulled up close enough to it that the passenger door could be opened for Cally to slip inside without being seen.

"Hey, Dad. Thanks again for doing this. You have power at the house?"

His father patted his son on the shoulder. "Of course, of course. Full power isn't up yet, but I'm told it'll be on within the hour or so. Our generator has plenty of juice left. I heard a thump. Did yours just conk out?"

"It did. Dad, this is Cally. Cally, this is my dad, the original Officer Thrace."

Cally came forward, and the appropriate introductions were made. Aaron felt queasy at the reality of involving his parents in a dangerous situation, but his father could handle it. Possibly better than he could. Will Thrace hadn't become a decorated officer for nothing.

"I'll come over as soon as Hatch arrives to relieve me," Aaron said, watching Cally ready herself to crawl into the back seat. A blanket lay folded in the center, the same gray color as the cushion fabric, to help camouflage her presence.

"Are you sure that's wise?" Concern filled every inch of Cally's face, and for some reason, it warmed Aaron from the inside. *She cares.*

"We'll do our base of operations switch first, then I'll be over. Should be around dinnertime, so it won't look suspicious for me to show up. I'd like to meet your uncle and do my own security sweep."

"My own son doesn't trust me," his father grumbled, but the comment held a teasing tone. "I know, I know. You have papers to fill out, personal reports, all that. I might miss being on the job sometimes, but that's one part of retirement I truly enjoy. Less paperwork."

Aaron touched Cally's sleeve. "Be careful. Stay low. I'll see you soon. And Leo should be dropping your uncle off there soon if he hasn't already."

Cally's worry shifted to a reserved smile. "Thanks."

He waited for her to turn around, to leave, but she remained motionless. When had they moved so close to each other? He could see the dark flecks in her eyes, every beautiful, black eyelash...

His father cleared his throat.

And then Cally slipped away to hide inside his parents' car, on the way to greater safety than he could provide for the time being.

Distracted and frustrated, he gathered up the necessary items to bring to another location—a building with lights on, at the very least. He'd be out of daylight and in total darkness inside the station within the hour.

He was zipping up a laptop bag at the front desk when he heard it—a rattling at the front doors. It sounded like someone was shaking the locked handles.

Aaron dropped into a crouch at the side of the desk as a shadowy shape released the handles and vanished around the edge of the building. Aaron's pulse sped up as he radioed his team.

"Potential intruder. Lights are out. Make it snappy, Hatch." The back door rattled. Then a side door.

The intruder was trying all the entrances. Were they truly that desperate that they'd attempt to break into a police station with armed officers?

One armed officer, he admitted. *And one who's been bested by their opponent so far.* Of course that would give a criminal a sense of confidence, regardless of whether that confidence was justified.

For a brief moment, Aaron considered opening the door and taking on his opponent—but what if things went wrong again? What if this time, it ended even worse for him?

His hand, which had been reaching for a side door that hadn't yet been tested by the intruder, pulled back.

I can't let that happen. For Cally's sake. She has endured enough loss already. I'll tackle this once I have backup.

The sound of breaking glass came from the other side of the building—and then a siren whooped as red and blue lights flashed outside to illuminate a thin, spry figure sprinting across police property. Aaron burst out of the building, weapon at the ready, but it was too late. The figure had vanished.

"Want me to go after him, boss?" Hatch climbed out of his vehicle, hand on his weapon.

"Yes, go."

Hatch climbed back into the vehicle and took off.

Had the individual figured out that the police station's power was completely out? It explained the boldness of the intrusion. But it also meant the person likely now knew the station had been abandoned.

Would the intruder deduce where Cally had gone, or had the culprit already known their plans and tried to enter the station in an attempt to reach her before she changed locations?

Aaron didn't want to waste time trying to determine the intruder's motivation... All he knew was that he needed to reach Cally before the attacker struck again.

Cally watched out the corner of the living room window at Aaron's parents' home, peeking through the gauzy fabric curtain. Their dog, the friendly German shepherd that Aaron had mentioned, sat beside her with her head shoved under Cally's fingers, begging for ear scratches. A patrol car pulled up to the driveway, and she was surprised to realize she recognized Aaron by his profile alone. Her heart spun in a quick circle as he exited the vehicle.

Why is this happening, God? All of it?

Aaron sauntered up the path, feigning a casual visit, but Cally didn't miss the tension in his neck and shoulders.

"Callandra," her uncle said, calling from the couch, "come have a seat and relax. Surely this isn't all as bad as you've said."

Her uncle Zarek had been dropped off by Leo at the Thrace home a few minutes before her, and while she'd tried her best to communicate the extent of the danger she'd faced for the past several days, he was having a difficult time fully comprehending the scenario he'd brought himself into.

"I've told you, it is. It's not that I don't want to spend

time with you—believe me, I'd rather have you here than anyone else in the family—but it's not safe. The best thing you could do to look out for me would be to charter a flight back first thing in the morning and spend some time at home appeasing my mother. Let her know I'm fine. You've seen me, the police are dealing with the situation and it's going to be okay."

But even as she said the words, she wasn't sure she believed them herself.

The front door opened, and Aaron came inside. She heard him stomping the snow off his boots down in the stairwell.

"If that's so, why are you pacing around like a nervous kitten? Sit down, relax. Aren't you boiling in that heavy sweater?" Uncle Zarek sighed pointedly. "Take it off, get comfortable. Tell you what, why don't we take a photo together to send your mom. That might calm her nerves a bit."

"Actually," Aaron said, entering the room, "I'm going to suggest we all move out of the living room, away from open windows. The basement and spare room on the south side of the house should be fine— just don't put yourself in direct line of sight to the outdoors."

The Thrace parents, who'd been elsewhere in the house, joined the trio in the living room. Cally backed away from the window immediately. "Why? I thought the whole point was that I'd be safe here. Has something happened?"

"Yes." Aaron looked like he wanted to say more, but spied the newcomer in the room for the first time. "Hi, you must be Zarek, Cally's uncle? I'm Aaron Thrace, Royal Canadian Mounted Police." The two men shook hands before Aaron continued. "Someone just tried to break into the police station. They didn't make it inside, but the intruder definitely knows the station is currently without power. At this point, we have to assume the individual has figured out there's no one left inside the station."

"So why are you here?" Aaron's father huffed. "Go after him!"

"First, I've been thinking about this, and…it might not have been a 'him.' Based on body type, we can't say if the person was male or female. Second, Hatch is on it. I sent him in pursuit. Third—" Aaron whipped his gaze around to lock eyes with Cally. Her heart did another pirouette as he took a step toward her. "I didn't want to leave you all alone."

"I'm not alone," she said, but could barely muster more than a whisper. His obvious concern for her was…alarming.

But not unwelcome.

And even after everything that had happened, that was the strangest part of it all.

At Aaron's insistence, his parents collected blankets, pillows and an air mattress, and set them up in the basement along with a pull-out couch. Apparently their basement guest room had recently been converted to a storage space, for which they apologized profusely before being shooed away by Aaron.

"Take the pullout, Uncle," Cally said, seeing the layout. "I'll use the air mattress, no problem." Uncle Zarek tried to insist otherwise, but Cally wouldn't let him win this one—she was younger, and her body could handle another night of rough sleep better than his. As she carefully set up the air mattress in a corner, she heard Aaron standing on the flight of stairs to the basement, trying to convince his parents to stay downstairs instead of returning to their own room for the night. It sounded as though his father was determined to remain upstairs. After several minutes, Aaron joined her and Uncle Zarek, looking flustered.

"They're staying upstairs. I can't convince them otherwise." He pointed to the small rectangular windows at the top of the basement wall, above the couch. "These windows are frosted, so as long as you don't open them, no one will know you're inside. Keep the lights off—use your phone flashlights if you need to, please. And if by chance there *is* trouble, I want you both to go to the furnace room and stay there until I've given an all clear that it's safe to come out."

"And what will *you* be doing?" Cally asked. "You can't spend another night awake. You've hardly slept the past two nights as it is."

And it showed, regardless of how much he protested. His eyes were bloodshot with dark circles underneath. He was going to such lengths for her, and she couldn't help feeling she wasn't worth it. That the risk and personal cost were too great.

Aaron shrugged. "I'm doing my job. I can rest when it's over."

His job. Of course. "It'll look great on your record if you can catch this attacker and make the town safe again by Christmas or sooner, I get that. But if you get sick or exhaustion causes you to get injured in the meantime, is that worth the risk?"

He sat down on the stairs and pressed the thumb and forefinger of his right hand into the corners of his eyes. "I was hoping that the risk would be worth a promotion, but that's not exactly looking promising any-more. I don't think I'll have this resolved by the tree lighting, and I can't apologize enough for that. I really wanted to make that happen for you."

She wasn't sure whether to feel grateful or guilty. "Is my being here costing you the chance of advance-ment in your job? Is that what's going on?"

He pulled his hand away and sat upright so fast she flinched back. "No! Of course not. That's not what I meant. I doubt I'd have even been considered a possi-bility for advancement in the first place if you hadn't decided to stay in Fort Mason—well, maybe eventu-ally, but...you know what, none of this is coming out correctly."

If the situation wasn't so serious, Cally would have giggled at the sudden, perplexed anguish on his face. It was strangely endearing. "I think that might have something to do with the lack of sleep."

"Ugh." He changed tactics and pressed the heels of his hands into his eyes instead. "Listen. You get the rest *you* need. And you're forgetting that Leo relieved me for a number of hours last night at the station. I might still have a mild sleep deficit, but I'm not running on empty. I'm going to spend the night right here on these stairs, where I can hear everything in the house and react as needed. If I start to nod off, Starbuck will wake me up—she's our first line of defense. Makes a great proximity alarm. Plus, if I know my dad, he'll try to relieve me in a few hours anyway."

Uncle Zarek sauntered over and tapped Cally on the arm. "Get some rest, Callandra. Get changed and go to bed. I'm sure things will look better in the morning." He suddenly grinned and whipped out his phone. "We didn't get to take that selfie for your mother, though! Now?"

Cally almost groaned, but she couldn't exactly say no. He made a good point, that it would calm her mother down. "All right."

Her uncle moved closer and wrapped his arm around her shoulders, then frowned. "Why are you still dressed like you're in the middle of a snowstorm? This house is nicely heated. Your mother will think you're living inside an igloo."

"Just press the button, Uncle," she said, but when he started to protest, she reached up and pressed the camera button for him. A semi-blurry photo appeared onscreen of the two of them, with half of Aaron's face at the edge of the picture. "Good enough."

Her uncle frowned again, looking nervous. "Callandra—"

She couldn't deal with this right now. Her uncle's insistence on sending a pleasant photo to her mother while people were actively trying to take her life was the strangest situation she'd found herself dealing with in a long time. "We'll take another one in the morning, all right? There'll be better lighting and it won't be blurry."

He sighed and busied himself on the phone for a moment before grunting as if frustrated.

Cally didn't want to take the bait, but she loved her uncle and, despite the inconvenience of his visit, was grateful that he cared enough to travel all this way to see her instead of returning home after what had likely been a draining business conference. "Is something wrong?"

Uncle Zarek pointed at his neck. "Your locket. Don't

tell me you've lost it?" His features pulled together sharply with worry. "Or stopped wearing it?"

"Oh!" She pulled on the chain and raised the metal oval from inside her layers of clothing. "No, it's still here, under everything. I'm not sure I'll ever stop wearing it. It's just easiest to keep it under all the fabric."

His relief was palpable. "Well. For a moment there…" His eyes flicked to Aaron and back to her. She swallowed hard on a sudden lump in her throat. The temperature in the room seemed to drop several degrees. What was he trying to imply?

"I'm not ever going to forget him," she said, her voice lowered to a near whisper. "No matter what happens or where life takes me. When you love someone, you love them always. That doesn't mean there isn't room for more love. It's not a finite resource."

"Oh, Callandra. That's not what I meant at all. I'm sorry." Uncle Zarek's face fell. "I…we'll talk in the morning. If you'd like, I can even polish it up for you, as its shine is looking a little dulled. All right?"

She nodded, suddenly unable to speak. As her uncle crawled beneath the blankets of the pull-out couch, her eyes heated up and began to water with emotion.

Aaron's hand landed on her arm. "Hey. Are you going to be okay? Is there anything I can do?"

There was. She just wasn't sure if he'd be open to it. "Can I…uh…sorry, this might sound really strange, but…"

The corner of his mouth lifted in a kind, understanding smile. "Did you want a hug?"

She did. So much.

With a quick nod, she fell into his open arms, feeling the safest she had since she'd stepped off the airplane two days ago.

"If you weren't playing bodyguard for me, what would you be doing right now?"

Aaron chuckled. "I'm not sure. Watching an action movie with Leo, usually, but he's kind of busy these days. Maybe reading some alternate history, or browsing for rescue dogs online."

Cally sat up and pulled back. "Really? I've always wanted a dog, but we only owned cats while growing up. I don't think I've ever read an alternate history book, either."

"History was my favorite school subject, believe it or not. If I wasn't in law enforcement, I'd probably be a high school history teacher. Or a full-time horse trainer. Or both."

Cally smiled and tucked back into his shoulder. "With a house full of rescue dogs?"

He laughed again. "Obviously. What about you? What would you be doing if you had an evening alone, danger-free?"

She thought of her couch at home, the warm blanket and pillows she'd longed for more than once since arriving in Fort Mason. "I'd be under a giant pile of blankets either reading or watching home renovation shows and knitting. I find it calming."

"I can understand that. You work from home, right? Must be difficult to relax and separate work from downtime."

"It is. But I can work from anywhere, which is nice. It gives me a lot of freedom, which opens up possibilities for the future in terms of expanding my client base, traveling, and so forth."

Aaron's arm tightened around her. "I'm in awe of people who are self-employed. It takes a lot of grit, determination and hustle to succeed and make a living, but the be-your-own-boss trade-off is appealing. You're a remarkable woman."

Her cheeks warmed at his words. She'd never heard anyone talk about her career aspirations with such understanding. The security and acceptance she found in his embrace was, in a way, alarming. She'd realized some time ago that her heart would let her know when it was ready to expand its capacity for love, to let someone else in and give back in return. But she certainly hadn't expected to feel its urging so soon.

And definitely not for a man whose life would only intertwine with hers for a short while.

Because despite his kindness, despite the hug, despite his fierce protection, he'd admitted as much tonight—she was a convenient circumstance to potentially advance his career. He hadn't meant it that way, but she'd read between the lines.

She wondered if he could read between hers...but she had a sneaking suspicion that at this very moment, as she clung to him and he pressed her cheek into his shoulder, they weren't even speaking the same language.

FOURTEEN

He hadn't expected her to fall asleep in his arms.

They sat side by side on the stairs, Cally one step above him with her head buried in the crook of his shoulder, and within minutes of holding her she'd fallen fast asleep. He was trying very hard not to be distracted by her beauty—by the rise and fall of each breath, by the way her lips parted ever so slightly. He wished he could reach inside of her and take away her pain, leaving behind only beautiful memories of the people she loved. He hoped that whoever captured her heart again—if ever she was willing to give it—respected those memories and allowed her to treasure them as much and as deeply as she needed to.

All he wanted was for her to find someone, or something, that made her smile again the way she was smiling in the photo tucked inside her locket. If she wanted to sit and tell him stories of her life with Esai, he'd gladly listen for hours. She deserved that much, after everything life had handed to her.

I can never be the one to make that happen, Lord, I know that. But won't You bring someone into her life who can?

As the night wore on, he flinched at every sound—the creaks of the house settling, the rustle of the dog turning over in her bed, the rap of the branches brushing the side of the house every time the wind gusted. He couldn't have fallen asleep even if he wanted to. Updates via text from Hatch let him know that the suspect who'd tried breaking into the station had escaped on a snowmobile—or at least that was Hatch's suspicion—which aligned with Aaron's belief that the culprit or culprits were getting around on these high-speed, off-road vehicles.

An update from Leo told him that his brother had been unable to interview the rental shop's owner last night—he was having trouble tracking down the man—but Leo was heading back to make another attempt first thing in the morning.

Speaking of morning, I also need to...

He closed his eyes for a moment, trying to think through the new information—and then startled back to wakefulness, immediately conscious of the fact that he'd fallen asleep on the stairs, Cally's head on his shoulder. And that there'd been no overnight attempt on their lives.

He extricated himself from Cally, carefully balling up his sweater to place it under her head so she could lean against the wall instead of his shoulder, and called his brother.

"I'm heading to the rental place right now," Leo said as soon as he answered. "I've got Hatch on welcome duty, since we have officials and officers arriving around noon. Power is back on throughout town, and back at the station, too. How'd the night shake out?"

"Surprisingly uneventful, if tense. Hang on, Hatch is calling us through the radio. Hatch, go ahead."

Even through the crackle of the radio speaker, Hatch's excitement was palpable. "Guys, you'll never guess what I just heard from Fort St. Jacob. They called to let me know they're on the way and we got to chatting—"

"The news, Hatch." Aaron heard a creak on the stairs and looked down to see Cally awake and standing, blinking the sleep out of her eyes.

"It's Tricia. Your Tricia, Aaron."

"She's not my Tricia, but that's irrelevant. What about her?" Aaron's insides tightened. "Has she been found?"

"Better and yet somehow worse," Hatch continued. "She's at the hospital in Fort St. Jacob. Her car went off the road last night, slid into the ditch and had to be towed out. Speed and alcohol might have been a factor, charges are pending. She's not seriously injured, but waiting in the ER to be checked over. Last I heard, she blew pretty close to the legal limit at the scene."

Aaron thanked his fellow officers, hung up and glanced at Cally. "You heard that, I assume."

She nodded, stretching her shoulders and arms. "I hope she's okay."

"Me, too."

"Is the tree lighting still happening tonight? I don't suppose I'll be going." She wrapped her arms across her stomach.

What's the right move here, Lord? "I'm honestly not sure." He crouched to scratch the dog, who'd wandered over, excited and happy that humans were finally waking up. "Here's where we're at. We know of one male involved in these attacks. Body type suggests there may be two people, but we can't say for certain. The only person we can pinpoint with a possible motive is Tricia, with jealousy as that motive, but the timeline doesn't really fit and she doesn't have a history of violence or priors on her record. Just…"

"Manipulation." Cally yawned. "You did say she's gone out of her way to interfere more than once when it comes to you and relationships, though you only told me the one story. It's the type of behavior that tends to get worse over time, until there's a breaking point— yours or theirs." She chuckled bitterly. "I hit mine with my family and flew to Canada for Christmas, but that's a different situation altogether."

"I have been thinking about this, and all I can manage is that it's *plausible* that Tricia organized the attacks against you. Not likely, but plausible, so it can't be ruled out. She might have learned via spa gossip that you were my assignment and grown concerned. Maybe that's a stretch, but I'm just thinking out loud here."

Cally tilted her head, looking much like the confused dog under his fingertips who'd grown concerned at the sudden lack of ear scratches. "Why would she fatally target me specifically, though? From what you've told me, her behavior up to this point has been more of a general 'keep you away from other women' mode of operating, which doesn't explain the level of violence toward *me*."

Aaron could have laughed aloud. "You're right. The targeting has been more general in the past, and this definitely isn't. But, Cally…you're a competent, self-employed, breathtakingly beautiful career woman who speaks…how many languages?"

"Oh! Five. But how—"

"The RCMP sent over a file on you with my assignment, but it's information easily found online. Tricia might have read up on you, seen your photo and grown concerned." When Cally didn't react, he took a deep breath and continued, about to say words filled with more honesty than she could ever know. "Concerned that I'd fall for you."

Her cheeks immediately flushed pink, a heart-stopping sight against her deep beige complexion. "Oh." She formed the word softly, eyes lowering for a single moment before snapping back up to meet his with a ferocity that demanded truth. "And have you?"

The world seemed to come to a standstill. Even the dog had grown quiet, as if everything hinged on this moment, on his answer to a simple question that really wasn't simple at all.

He didn't know why Cally had come into his life. Why God had sent this woman whose life was worlds away, but with whom he felt a connection unlike with any other person he'd met before. He didn't know if answering with the truth would bring joy or pain, but he did know that he absolutely, unequivocally, could not lie.

"Yes," he said, and she gasped. "Moment by moment."

Her lips parted as if she didn't know how to respond, and the silence stabbed at him in a way he hadn't anticipated. How could her reply to his confession matter *so much* when he hadn't ever expected to even admit his feelings to her in the first place?

"Aaron," she finally said, and he braced himself

for the twist of the knife. She took a step closer. He couldn't remember how to breathe. "Me, too."

Now what? She couldn't believe she'd said it and admitted to herself, let alone the man in front of her, that she was actually falling for a Mountie.

She'd expected him to say no to her question, to laugh and shrug it off and tell her they needed to get back to business. But he hadn't, and that made everything both relieving and terrifying at the same time.

"What are we going to do?" she murmured. He hadn't moved or breathed since her own admission.

His answer was resolute. "Nothing." Her heart sank, and it must have shown on her face because he exclaimed with alarm. "Oh! No, not...that's not what I mean. Right now, nothing. Later, something. But right now, Cally, I have to focus on keeping you safe so that we *can* do something about it."

She exhaled with relief. "Of course. So, without a culprit in custody...do I go to the tree lighting tonight or not?"

Aaron sighed and glanced out the front window. The weather appeared to have grown milder overnight— the trees were still and no more snow fell from the sky. Cally thought she even saw a patch of blue poking through the perpetual gray.

"Here's the dilemma," he said. "Either you stay here alone with my father—who is a capable former officer, mind you—or you hole up in the station with Hatch, or I bring you to the tree lighting, where you'll be in public, fully visible and surrounded by twelve armed RCMP officers in a controlled area. If a civilian tries to pull a weapon on you in the middle of the town square…like I said, there are twelve armed officers scheduled to be there, some of them mounted on horseback, plus there's typically a minimum of five hundred attendees. My professional opinion is that it will be safer for you in public with law enforcement around than sitting in a building with one other person, but I won't force you to go if you're concerned."

Cally's insides roiled. The thought of walking out into the open after everything that had happened seemed more frightening than she'd anticipated—but Aaron knew what he was talking about. She trusted him. He wouldn't put her in intentional danger. *He's falling for me.*

That still threw her for a loop.

The more she thought about the tree lighting, and the more she envisioned staying inside the house while the town and the public's focus was elsewhere, the more her nerves flared. Even going to the police station seemed like an unwelcome alternative. After all, Tricia had waltzed right inside the police station, and she'd seemed perfectly normal until Cally knew the whole story—and then Tricia had become a suspect and vanished. Even if Tricia wasn't involved, what would stop someone else from trying the same trick to get close to her? Especially if the person knew she was in the station and that every officer save one was manning the event in the middle of town?

Safety was relative, no matter where she went.

She planted her hands on her hips with firm resolve, her body stiff and shaky after a long night on the stairs drifting in and out of sleep.

"All right," she said. "I trust you. You were chosen

to protect me for a reason, because the people who gave you this assignment trust *you*. Let's go to the square."

Was she still afraid? Of course. But with Aaron and his colleagues looking out for her, she had faith that everything was going to be okay.

She desperately hoped her faith wasn't misplaced.

FIFTEEN

Aaron stood in the town square with his arm around Cally, who shrank against him. She'd seemed so confident until they'd stepped outside, and though he'd given her the option of returning to his parents' house or the station, she'd declined. He wanted nothing more than to prove the trust she'd given him was not misplaced.

The Fort Mason town square was packed with attendees. More folks from the surrounding area had driven up to take part in the festivities than he'd anticipated at the beginning of the week, when the weather was awful. But after a day filled with sunshine and with the snow glistening as early twilight descended, the scene was a stark contrast to the stormy, abandoned streets of only a few days prior. Aaron could almost imagine what it would be like to enjoy the tree lighting rather than be standing on high alert, watchful and waiting just in case Cally's attacker—or attackers—decided to reveal themselves. But the uncertainty was beyond frustrating.

Five RCMP officers were stationed at various points around the square on horseback, and some locals had hitched up their own horses and wagons to offer hayrides to families around the area. Stores, poles, signs and everything in between were decorated in red and green garlands and white lights. Tinsel wreaths of lights, stars and trees hung from the lampposts.

The central focus, the main reason for the gathering, was the giant tree in the center of the square. It stood almost three stories tall, and every year a local community group had a friendly competition to see which one got to head out into the woods, find and decorate the tree. The men's hockey scrimmage team had won the privilege this time, and they'd done a fantastic job. In previous years, there'd been a flashing lights show, a white-lights-only aesthetic, and a children's tree decorated with fake candles and paper lanterns folded by kids from across the province—and every year, the lights came on after sundown at exactly five o'clock.

"You doing okay?" He glanced at Cally. Her shoulders appeared less tense than when they'd first arrived, but her eyes still darted around from person to person. She appeared to be scanning the crowd, worriedly searching for a familiar face, but with her Uncle Zarek by her side, too, she'd begun to move away from Aaron rather than stay tucked quite so close. It surprised Aaron how much loss he felt at the simple shift in spacing between their bodies.

"I'm actually feeling a lot better," she said. "Ellen came up with her brother, right? I meant to arrange a meeting point with her, but got caught up in my own anxiety."

"I'm sure she understands," he said. "Jamie had to set up some of the detour signs around town, so she's probably helping him if you haven't heard from her." She nodded in response, but her gaze still looked distant and worried. He scoured his brain for a suggestion that might ease her mind. "Hey, let's stand over by Leo and Zephyr. She's a sweetheart of a horse. You can give her a scratch if you want, and I suspect Leo has some treats in his pocket. Horse isn't one of the languages you speak, is it?"

Cally snorted with sudden laughter. The sound warmed his insides as if he'd drank an entire vat of hot cocoa. *That* was what he wanted for her. Happiness, unexpected moments of joy. And despite their admission that morning that they'd begun to fall for each other, it guaranteed nothing. Would they keep in touch once she went back to Amar? Were these feelings even worth exploring? Long-distance relationships were difficult at best, impossible at worst. Even with all the social media apps available to connect through, it would make his heart ache to see her updates and photos, knowing they were so many worlds apart from each other.

Wait, heartache? The realization startled him. Were his feelings stronger than he'd thought? Could he actually be falling...in *love*?

He'd never felt for anyone the way he felt for Cally. He'd never entertained notions of the future with a woman the way he couldn't help but do when it came to her. Even with Tricia, his heart had found excuses and reasons why a romantic relationship wouldn't work out. With Cally, his heart and mind kept racing through ways that it could.

If that meant he was in love, well...he needed to think about it some more. Later, when he wasn't in the middle of protective detail after several days of intense danger. He tried to refocus his thoughts as Cally's uncle shifted closer, looking around the crowd with almost as much intensity as Cally—and while technically Cally was Aaron's only assignment, he couldn't help but suspect that the spirit of his protective detail orders included her family member, as well.

Aaron tried to help the man feel at ease. "Sir, Cally mentioned you work for the Department of Natural Resources in Amar, but that sounds like government business. Holding an international conference so close to Christmas seems unusual."

"It is, it is, believe me." The man rolled his eyes. "But there's a bill that our government is trying to push through in regard to some reserve areas and the country's oil—I'm sure you've heard of our booming oil industry of the past few years? There were some experts gathering from Alberta, Texas, Amar and Saudi Arabia to do some emergency examinations of new science and new technologies that should help all of us. It's not an ideal time of year, but we manage for the good of our countries."

"That's very generous of everyone involved, I'm sure." Aaron's radio buzzed with the chatter of fellow RCMP officers, each person checking in at a designated time. His time was in five minutes, which meant the lighting was about ten minutes away. He needed to get in position and ensure that Cally was secure—and hopefully able to see the tree. Despite the danger and fear she'd endured so far during this visit, he could at least give Cally one positive experience by which to remember their town. Especially since the danger wasn't over—not by any means.

He brushed her elbow. "Can you see all right from

here?" Though the tree was big enough to rise high into the air, she wasn't a tall woman.

"I'm fine, thank you for checking." Her smile was gentle and sincere. "I know you said there'd be a large turnout, but I'm still impressed."

Her uncle huffed and clicked his tongue. "Cally, dear niece, I love you, but you're as small as a kitten and there's no way you can see anything but the very tip of the tree. You're special enough to get a personal RCMP escort—shouldn't you have a VIP view of the event?"

She pursed her lips, and Aaron recognized the gesture as a strong effort on her behalf to clamp down a wave of frustration. "No, Uncle. That's quite all right."

"Don't be foolish. I'll head up front with you so you can see better."

"I don't think that's such a good idea." Cally looked over to Aaron for support.

Aaron shook his head. "No, it's safest for Cally to remain here. If we'd organized it a few minutes ago, that'd be different, but it's too late to rearrange—"

Zarek snorted. "The lights are coming on at any second, yes? Surely we can go up there for a moment. Escort us up if you want. I can see a VIP area with town officials and such."

As frustrating as the request was, Aaron didn't want to treat the man with disrespect. He pulled out his radio to see if there was a possibility of moving Zarek and Cally up safely before the lights came on. "Thrace to Biers, is there any way we can move two VIPs up before—"

"Uncle, no! We have to wait—" Cally's shout yanked his focus, but he was too late. The edges of Cally's and Zarek's coats disappeared into the crowd.

"Wait, sir! Stop!" He bolted after them into the crowd, but couldn't see either of them through the packed square. As quickly as the crowd parted to let someone through, it closed up again like water filling in the sides of a container.

He'd nearly reached the front when a gasp arose from the crowd. The lights of the tree began to glow, bright white and gleaming in sequence as they spiraled around the tree. Instrumental carols piped into the square through speakers set up at the corners, the illumination matching the rise and fall of the music. Small globe ornaments pulsed to the beat, which would be quite impressive—under different circumstances.

Cally's need to escape made even greater sense now. It wasn't that her family did these kinds of things out of malice; they just had little concept of her autonomy. It was probably made even worse by the loss of her husband—they likely saw her as vulnerable and in need.

With everyone staring at the tree, it grew even more difficult to break through the crowd. People were reluctant to move aside because they were busy watching, and no matter how loud Aaron yelled for the crowd to make way for law enforcement, his voice battled the volume of the music coming from the speakers surrounding the area.

After what felt like ages, he emerged at the front, anticipating a clueless Uncle Zarek and an aggravated Cally standing at the edge of the VIP section.

But they were nowhere to be seen.

Aaron opened a channel on his radio. "Does anyone have eyes on Cally and Zarek? He is wearing a navy blue coat, she is wearing a puffy gray coat and white knit hat."

Fellow officers around the square chimed in with negative responses as the tree's lighting sequence finished. A cry of appreciation rose up from the crowd, the applause loud and the cheers deafening. Any other year, the happiness of the townsfolk and visitors would have made Aaron smile and feel a rush of gratitude for the season and sense of community spirit.

Right now, however, all he felt was frustration and a sinking sense of defeat.

With the lighting sequence over and the second half of the festivities about to begin, the crowd started to disperse, clumping and moving apart like a storm surge. He got on his radio to give instructions to the other officers stationed around the square.

Lord, help me search. Keep her safe.

He circled the perimeter, shouting communications over the radio and listening for updates, the seconds ticking by like hours.

No one had seen them.

And then Aaron found himself standing in an empty section of the square, alone.

Despite all their planning, all the officers, all the reassurances he'd given her that she'd be safe…Cally had vanished without a trace.

His radio buzzed. With his body on autopilot, he pressed the button to answer the call.

"Thrace? It's Biers. I have news from Fort. St. Jacob. That Tricia woman left the hospital in Fort St. Jacob an estimated few hours ago, maybe two? The hospital has been so busy, they didn't notice until about twenty minutes ago. She fled the ER, and the police don't know where she's gone."

The radio tumbled from Aaron's hand.

* * *

Why am I so cold? Cally shivered, the side of her head pounding as if she had a migraine. But she didn't get migraines, so why did her head hurt? She tried to open her eyes, but all she could see was a sea of black and white sparks. As her vision slowly cleared, she focused on the sound of shuffling feet and the sensation of tugging on her wrists.

I can't move my arms.

The realization startled her to full consciousness. Snow swirled around her, falling from the tree branches overhead—trees that surrounded her on all sides. She was in the woods...at night?

"Aaron?" She tested her voice, relieved to find it working without issue. "Uncle Zarek?"

That was when she noticed movement at the edge of her vision. Uncle Zarek was beside her, tying off the edge of a rope that wound around her wrists and ankles.

"Uncle? What are you doing?" A horrifying notion began to dawn, but she refused to entertain it just yet. "Why are you doing this? There are people after me, people who—"

Her uncle stepped back, his work finished. His eyes glistened with unshed tears, but Cally didn't buy his display of emotion for one second. He needed to explain himself first.

"I have no choice," he pleaded, palms facing up, open and vulnerable. "You leave me no other option. I promise, Callandra, I'm not trying to hurt you. I'm trying to save you."

She stared at him. What on earth was her uncle talking about? He made no sense. "If you're not trying to hurt me, let me go." She tugged at her bonds. "This isn't going to save me. You know there are people trying to kill me, and you'll be handing me over to them like this."

Had Aaron noticed she was missing? He was probably frantically searching for her. Her memories of being pulled into the crowd by her uncle were fuzzy, but she thought she vaguely recalled resisting and trying to yank her arm away when he'd insisted they leave the square.

She wanted to ask him about it, but pain shot through her skull every time she moved her head to one side. She hissed at the sharp sensation.

"You hit your head on one of the speaker stands," Uncle Zarek said, anticipating her question. "I didn't do that to you. The speaker fell over when you bumped into it, and I slipped us away when an officer came by to help set it right. Please don't think poorly of me. I'm doing everything I can to keep you alive."

She was tugging on the ropes again, ready to scream for help, when he stepped forward, grabbed the sides of the chain around her neck and gave them a sudden downward jerk. The clasp snapped open and Zarek pulled the chain and locket into his palm.

"No!" Cally strained and thrashed, ignoring the way the ropes bit into her wrists. "What are you *doing*?"

"Shh!" He placed his finger on his lips. "Callandra. I need you to listen very carefully. I never intended for you to get hurt, and I need you to believe that I'm doing everything I can to prevent further harm from coming your way. I've been trying to keep you safe since the moment your mother told me you'd unexpectedly run off and boarded a plane bound for Canada."

"But—"

"Shh!" The panic and fear that flashed across his face stunned her into silence. "Please. Keep quiet and don't try to follow me. As soon as I'm far enough away from you, I'll call the police and tell them where you are. I'm sure that kind officer who has eyes for you will love the chance to play the hero. But until then, please stay quiet and hidden. There are some very dangerous people on their way to meet me—well, you've already met them, and their actions have been outside of the boundaries of our agreement, believe me—who will not hesitate to get what they want. They appear to have some very mistaken notions regarding your involvement in my business."

Business? "Uncle, what are you talking about? What business?"

"They've paid a lot of money for some very privileged information, and think you..." He closed his fist around the locket and squeezed his eyes shut. "I'm sorry. I'm so sorry."

He turned on his heel and ran, heading through the trees. Cally thought she heard the rumbling of a car engine in the distance. Had her uncle stolen someone's car, too?

"Wait!" she shouted at the top of her lungs, her throat already feeling the strain. Despite his instructions to stay still and quiet, she had more self-preservation than to stand in the middle of a snow-filled forest, tied to a fence where she'd slowly freeze to death. The air already felt several degrees colder than when she'd left the Thraces' home to head to the tree lighting, which didn't bode well for the hours ahead.

Why would her uncle take her locket? What was he talking about—what business? Her throat tightened and a hiccup threatened to send her emotions into overdrive.

I need to focus. I can react later, once I'm safe and warm and no bad guys are searching for me.

She inhaled slowly, then took a closer look at the ropes around her wrists and ankles—and noticed how poorly they were tied. Her uncle hadn't been wearing gloves, so his fingers had likely grown cold and cramped, especially during his attempt to tie her ankles to the fence. He'd have had to plunge his hands directly into the snow.

With a cry of triumph, Cally wiggled her arms and legs, pulling harder and twisting her wrist and ankle joints to maneuver her way out. Within seconds, she'd pulled her feet out of her boots and freed one of her hands. It took a few more seconds to free her dominant hand, pull her boots out from under the ropes and slide her frozen toes back inside.

And then she ran.

She found the road easily, but without lights to illuminate the way, it was difficult to see which direction she should be heading. She thought she saw the black outline of a road sign in the distance, but until she reached it, she wouldn't know if she was actually making her way back to town or heading farther away.

"Help!" she shouted as she jogged, mindful of conserving energy but also deeply concerned at the possibility of spending the night outside. She had to keep moving or she'd freeze.

Her stomach lurched with anxiety as headlights appeared in the distance. Friend or foe? How much weight should she give her uncle's words about trying to divert the people after her onto himself...or were his actions and theirs even related? How did her uncle and Tricia know each other? *What business?*

She didn't even realize she'd started crying until the tracks of her tears turned cold.

The car quickly came closer, and she made a decision. While staying on the road and flagging down the car *might* be unsafe, staying outside in the freezing temperatures overnight was a *guaranteed* danger.

Okay, God. I want to learn to trust You again. Please give me strength.

She raised her arms and ran along the side of the road toward the oncoming car, praying the driver would stop and not ignore her. The closer the car came, the more she worried that she'd made a terrible mistake—

And then the car's tires skidded on the snow and ice, and lights on the roof began to flash red and blue, and Cally's relief was so immense that she started to laugh and cry at the same time.

The driver's-side door flew open and Aaron burst out. He ran toward her and they collided, his arms wrapping around her in the strongest hug she'd ever received in her entire life.

"I don't think I've ever been so glad to see anyone," she said, her voice muffled by his heavy RCMP jacket.

"I could say the same." His breath came heavier than hers, and she had a sudden realization—the man was trying not to cry.

She leaned away and gazed up at him. "I'm okay. You're here and I'm okay. But my uncle isn't. This is his doing. All of it."

Aaron stared at her, lips parted, clearly trying to process her words. "He's…what?"

"He stole my locket. He didn't explain it very well

but said something about dangerous people who'd paid a lot of money and trying to protect me. That harming me wasn't part of the deal, whatever that means."

"Do you know where he went?"

Cally shook her head. "He said he'd call the police as soon as he was far enough away from me. He evidently thinks he's going to escape quickly, with no one able to follow and catch him. Maybe the airport? That's the only place I can think of that he'd be able to disappear fast without someone being able to follow, especially if there's a charter plane waiting for him. I don't get it. He's not thinking straight. But I am."

Before Aaron could say anything else, before he could protest and tell her that it wouldn't work out between them, she planted her hands on Aaron's shoulders, launched herself up to her tiptoes and pressed her mouth against his.

SIXTEEN

Aaron couldn't believe this was happening—and he also couldn't believe it was over so quickly.

He stared as Cally pulled away, a hint of a smile on her face. "Thank you for coming to rescue me," she said. "How did you know where to find me?"

"I didn't," he said, but his words were breathless and forced. Had she honestly just *kissed* him? "I…the RCMP set up barriers at the town limits, but I had a funny feeling that if you'd been taken, you'd be past the town limits already. I prayed for God's guidance, and for whatever reason, I had a sense of peace when I decided to travel the same road to the airport that we've taken a few times before. And then I saw you running toward me."

He embraced her again, wishing that the whole situation was resolved already so he could stand here and hold her forever—but as he released her, ready to ask her about the kiss, the radio in the patrol car beeped. "I need to check that," he said. Cally didn't hesitate; she nodded and followed him to the car.

They slipped inside, and he opened the channel before he'd even made it all the way into his seat. "Go ahead."

"Hey, it's Leo. I just heard back from the rental place about the snowmobile—actually, I had to track the owner down at the tree lighting. I guess he's on the volunteer crew, one of the hockey guys, so he's been tough to get in touch with."

Aaron pulled the car onto the road and put the call on speaker, bracing himself for more bad news. "Give it to me."

"A man rented the snowmobile and wanted to pay in cash, but that made the owner nervous so he insisted the guy leave a physical address to comply with the permits and so forth. He made a copy of the guy's class five license, but it wasn't until after the man left that the owner realized the individual had used a forged ID and given him the address of that cop motel outside of Fort St. Jacob. You know, the one on the highway between St. J's and Schroeder Lake."

"Any video footage?"

"Nothing useful. Black-and-white and grainy. I saw some stills via cell phone camera, and honestly the guy looks like the one you described after the attack in the grocery store. I'm sending over the image right now, but this might explain why we're having trouble with the townsfolk giving us any assistance. We're asking the wrong townsfolk."

Aaron wanted to punch the steering wheel. So the person or people responsible—and he wasn't going to pin this on anyone specific just yet, he didn't have enough evidence—had stayed outside of town, made lengthy trips up to Fort Mason on a snowmobile and back roads to avoid getting caught, and then…crashed their snowmobile? "Did he only rent one?"

"No, that's just it. The guy paid a hefty sum to rent two, but only left one name. And the owner only ever saw one person. Which, yes, also illegal, but we'll deal with that later."

"Thanks, Leo. Keep the channels open. I'm pursuing a lead at the regional airport and it's entirely possible that—"

The radio suddenly buzzed with static, as if they'd entered a dead zone for reception—not unusual out on the back roads, especially during the winter. Aaron would simply wait for reception to return so he could continue to update Leo and the rest of the force, until—

Something slammed into the side of the vehicle.

Cally screamed as the patrol car slid sideways on the snowy road. Despite having been plowed and salted, there was still plenty of snow and ice on the road underneath the tires, and the car spun as Aaron tried to correct their course. When he managed to get the car reoriented, he saw it. A snowmobile sat in the road in front of them, the front end looking dinged but not much worse for wear. The driver, suited in full black gear, likely hadn't intended to damage their snowmobile—just make a serious effort to force the patrol car off the road.

Well, it hadn't worked. And it wouldn't. No one was going to scare him away from getting to that airport and, Lord willing, getting some answers. It was time to finish this.

The snowmobile driver revved his vehicle. His opponent wanted to play chicken on winter roads? Aaron knew how this worked, and he refused to be intimidated.

He stepped on the gas and the patrol car zoomed forward, directly at the oncoming driver.

Cally braced herself, one hand on the side of her seat and the other on the handle above the door. The instant before impact, the snowmobile driver yanked his wheel and spun the skis of his off-road vehicle, sliding horizontally in front of the patrol car and sending sprays of snow shooting up in front of the windshield.

Aaron shouted in alarm but slammed on the brakes for a split second before charging ahead.

In the side mirror, Cally saw the snowmobile slip around to the back of the patrol car, then race up the side. The driver withdrew a long-barreled black handgun and aimed it toward the patrol car.

"Aaron! He's going to shoot at us!"

"I see it. Stay braced, this is going to get wobbly for a minute."

The moment the words left his mouth, he pulled the steering wheel to the left ever so slightly, then pushed it to the right just as the snowmobile driver came up parallel to the patrol car's back wheels, angling the gun as if to fire through the back window.

Aaron's maneuver sent the front end of the car veering right, cutting off the snowmobile driver and sending his shot wide. Cally ducked out of instinct, and in the side mirror she saw the driver plummet into the ditch and tip sideways. Relief filled her veins as Aaron corrected the patrol car's trajectory and kept going.

"Well, I guess that tells us something," he mumbled, sounding angry.

"There's definitely more than one person involved in this," she said. "I don't know where my uncle fits in, but we know he only just arrived yesterday, right? His attendance at the conference is traceable. But if there were two snowmobiles rented…that man who attacked at the spa, and…Tricia? I don't understand how my uncle and Tricia fit together, or what my locket has to do with anything. None of this makes sense. And how does my uncle even think he's going to take off from the airport, if that's where he is? It doesn't operate after four o'clock!"

"It operated last night by federal order when your uncle headed up here," he reminded her. "I guess with everything going on, it's entirely plausible that someone might have posed as law enforcement to get the same thing to happen tonight. Or threw money at an attendant and bribed them to keep the place open. Or they could simply be using the runways unauthorized."

Cally swallowed hard on a lump in her throat. Had her uncle been telling the truth, that he'd been trying to protect her from the attackers? But his actions betrayed his words, despite the fear he'd shown.

The tension in the vehicle ratcheted up as they pulled onto the long road leading into the airport. Cally felt her shoulders creep up around her ears, her neck tightening with unshakable stress as Aaron parked the car thirty meters from the door. He radioed in to his fellow officers, and Cally gasped when she realized that the front door to the airport was open. There appeared to be a light on inside.

"I'm going in," she said, unbuckling her seat belt.

"No, you're not," Aaron replied. He climbed out of the car and slammed the door—and locked it.

Cally tried the door. It didn't budge. She pounded on the window and shouted at Aaron, but still it remained locked. How could he do this to her? How could he keep her inside? Her uncle was in there, she needed answers—

Aaron slipped into the airport.

Seconds later, the car door unlocked.

She didn't waste a single second. She burst out of the car and ran at top speed toward the open door.

SEVENTEEN

For a moment, Aaron wasn't entirely sure what he was looking at. From where he stood inside the doorway, he could see into the waiting room of one of the airport gates. Half of the terminal was still dark, as if someone had only turned on the lights they needed. When Aaron stuck his head around the corner of the waiting area, he saw no one else. The airport felt as empty as the night Cally had been left behind, so he'd unlocked the doors of the patrol car via remote so Cally could come inside instead of wait in the vehicle all alone and risk triggering a terrible flashback to when she'd been by herself and threatened inside the police car two days before.

Aaron reached the front door at the same moment Cally burst inside.

"Did you find him? My uncle?" Cally's gaze darted frantically around the terminal. "I didn't see a car outside. I should have mentioned, he must have stolen a car to get here, but wouldn't we see it in the front lot? He might not even be here—"

A door banged on the other side of the terminal. It came from the direction of the washrooms, and Aaron could have kicked himself—why hadn't he thought to check there first? This had the potential to be a repeat of Cally's first incident all over again.

A familiar voice boomed out of the darkness.

"Hang on…what is this? Why…?" Uncle Zarek emerged from the washroom, straightening his suit jacket. When he noticed Aaron and Cally, he did a double take right before a look of horror washed over his face. "No…no! You can't be here! Callandra, I told you to stay away from me. You need to hide, quickly!"

Aaron's hands found his Taser. He slid it quietly out of its holster.

"Sorry, what?" Zarek scurried toward the open front door, but Aaron raised his weapon.

"Stop right where you are. What's going on? Why did you kidnap your niece?"

Zarek turned around slowly, his hands in the air. One of his fists was clenched shut. "Please, listen to me. You need to hide. Go in the washroom or out the back, or in the luggage room. Anywhere, and do it quickly. They'll be here any second."

"Who?" Cally pleaded with her uncle and moved closer to Aaron's side, and he could almost feel the confusion and fear radiating off her. "Where's Tricia? What role does she play in all this?"

Her uncle frowned. "Who's Tricia?"

And then Aaron heard it—the buzz of a snowmobile coming closer.

Zarek's confusion turned to panic. "You're too late. They'll see the patrol car and know you're here, and I won't be able to save you. I'll try." He looked at Cally with sadness and determination. "I wasn't lying when I said that's what I've been trying to do this whole time.

I never meant for things to go this far. Please believe me. That's why I came. I was going to come anyway, but you gave me an excuse. I—"

A shot rang out. Cally screamed as her uncle fell face-first onto the ground, and Aaron switched out his weapon and drew his sidearm as a person in white winter gear and a white helmet strode through the open door, gun extended and aimed at the two of them. Aaron had had no time to make a plan, no time to figure out what was going on.

"Get behind me," Aaron murmured to Cally. She complied.

The white-suited figure tilted his head at Aaron and Cally, shaking his weapon and shouting angrily beneath his helmet. Aaron couldn't make sense of the words—it sounded like their attacker was speaking another language. Before Aaron could protest his lack of understanding, Zarek groaned from the floor. The armed attacker looked down and crouched, weapon still trained on Aaron and Cally.

He reached for Zarek's clenched fist and pulled something out of the center—*the locket*. Weapons at a stalemate, the man then backed out of the airport instead, shutting the door behind him.

It made sense—Aaron figured he would have done the same thing. If one of them had fired, they'd have both lost.

But that didn't mean Aaron was going to let him get away. The instant the door closed, he sprang toward it, trying to shake it open as Cally rushed over to assist her uncle.

Uncle Zarek moaned. Aaron looked over his shoulder and winced as blood seeped out from under the man's body. Cally appeared to be dialing 911, and Aaron didn't have the heart to tell her that help might not arrive in time.

"What just happened?" Cally cried as she waited for the call to connect.

Aaron slammed his fists against the door, launching his weight into the crash bar. "There's something inside the locket. Your uncle has gotten himself mixed up in a very dangerous scheme, Cally. I can almost guarantee it."

"But he said he was trying to protect me…and the attacker, he yelled at me, he said…" Her voice trailed off.

Aaron wasn't going to stand around and wait for Cally's attacker to disappear again—he decided to take a page out of the criminal's book.

He grabbed one of the chairs in the waiting area and hurled it with all his strength at the front windows. The chair crashed through the nearest pane, providing Aaron with an opening to leap through, weapon drawn. Halfway down the driveway, a black-suited figure revved a snowmobile as the first assailant raced toward it.

"They're going to get away!" Cally's voice filled with dismay behind him.

"Not if I can help it," Aaron said. So there were two assailants after all—two people who'd bested him so far, thanks to the element of surprise. But this time, he had the advantage, and an even stronger motivation.

These villains needed to be served justice for all the suffering and harm they'd done to the woman he loved.

He dropped into fighting stance, then raised his sidearm—but as the first assailant reached the moving snowmobile and climbed aboard, both he and the snowmobile driver raised their weapons, as well. Two armed assailants against one.

What do I do, Lord?

"Aaron! Unbalance them!" Cally shouted behind him.

Aaron grunted. "You're absolutely right."

Sirens rose in the distance.

He lowered his aim and took the shot—at the snowmobile's engine.

Three rounds slammed into the front of the vehicle. The snowmobile lurched, skidded sideways and pitched onto its side, trapping the passengers underneath.

Police cars careened into the airport driveway, lights flashing as they sped toward the downed snowmobile. The attackers were trying to pull themselves out from under the heavy vehicle, to make an escape—but it was too late. Officers poured out of the cars with weapons drawn. The snowmobile driver raised his weapon, too, in a last-ditch attempt at resistance.

Aaron saw it coming before it happened. He spun around and reached through the empty window for Cally, pulling her face into his shoulder as his fellow officers raised their sidearms and multiple bangs split the air.

The sound echoed into silence and Cally drew back. "Is it over?"

He nodded, sad for the inevitable loss of life but relieved that the danger to Cally was finally over. "I think so." Then he glanced back at Uncle Zarek. "But not quite. I've got to get these doors braced so the paramedics can come inside." He struggled with the doors, managing to swing them open and hold them in place with door stoppers. As the paramedics rushed in with a stretcher and equipment, Aaron found Cally standing stock-still, staring at the huddled mass of people around the one relative she'd thought she could trust.

His heart ached for her.

He placed his hand on her shoulder. She flinched, startled out of her own thoughts. "You should sit down," he said. "We'll get our answers, but in the meantime, the paramedics are going to do everything they can. We're going to get your uncle the medical attention he needs. That comes first. All right?"

She nodded, clearly in too much shock to speak. It looked like the words kept slipping from her lips every time she tried to shape them, and Aaron wished he knew what to say to make things better—or whether he shouldn't say anything at all.

So he tried that first, leaning over to plant a gentle, soft kiss on her waiting mouth.

When he pulled back, her features had relaxed, but worry still ringed her eyes. And when she spoke his name, the timbre was scratchy and uncertain. "Aaron?"

"Yes?" He took her hand to encourage her, but her breathing had gone shallow.

"We *have* all the answers we need. The guy who yelled at us under his helmet? He was speaking Amaran. Not English. This entire time, it's had nothing to do with Tricia at all. My uncle must have been using me to move information by hiding it inside my locket— what my uncle said to me earlier makes sense now. When the guy came into the airport yelling at us, he was saying something about me wanting to be cut in on their deal, accusing me of running away to try to delay the information transfer so I could demand more money or blackmail them. That means…that means my uncle has been deceiving me since day one. Since the day of Esai's memorial. The one family member I thought I could trust has been betraying me this entire time."

A sob escaped her lips, the weight of truth visibly bearing down on her.

"Aaron," she said, gazing up at him. He'd thought he'd never seen a greater sadness on anyone in his lifetime.

"Tell me what I can do," he said. "Anything. How can I help?"

She shook her head, tiny shakes like vibrations that resonated through her entire body.

"I don't know," she said. "I don't know if there's anything *to* do. I don't know how I've been so blind. Or how God could have allowed this to happen. Aaron…I don't know if I can ever trust anyone again."

EIGHTEEN

The afternoon of Ellen's wedding, Cally sat in her uncle's hospital room for her daily visit. She had a few free hours between the ceremony and the reception while the bride and groom were taking photos, and since she didn't think she'd have a chance to visit after the event, she'd decided to stop in for a little while. Uncle Zarek had needed surgery on his spine to remove the bullet and repair damaged vertebrae, but it was going to be a long road to recovery and the doctors weren't sure he'd ever walk again. A few days ago, he'd been moved from ICU to a regular hospital surgical bed to begin some passive mobility exercises. Soon the hospital would be moving him to a rehab unit for a few weeks.

And though it had been a week since she'd learned of her uncle's betrayal, every part of Cally's body still ached at his admission. She didn't know how she was going to tell her mother, let alone the rest of the family. She'd spoken on the phone with various relatives in vague terms, but she hadn't truly processed the situation enough in her own mind to relay it with accuracy to everyone else. Plus, it seemed like a conversation best held in person when she returned to Amar after Christmas.

It wasn't that she didn't know the details—she had all of them, perhaps more than she needed. The paramedics had rushed Uncle Zarek to the hospital for surgery, and as soon as he'd woken up and shaken off the effects of the anesthesia, Cally had gone in to speak with him. Aaron and another officer had coached her on what to say, and how to shape her questions to encourage a confession of the truth.

But he'd told her everything, and she hadn't even needed to ask.

It turned out her uncle had a spending problem—his government job for the Department of Natural Resources had sent him around the world, given him many opportunities, but it had also caused him to start looking at the world in terms of what he *didn't* have. Fancy cars like the representative from Switzerland had. A gorgeous house in the country like the one owned by a British representative he'd met at a conference. Expensive clothes, luxurious vacations. His government job didn't pay a whole lot, and he'd started seeing cracks in the system.

With the influx of money to Amar after the oil discovery, he and the other employees had waited and waited for some of the benefits to start to pour down to them. The country was getting richer, his relatives were getting richer, and his department had expected to see rapid improvement, forgetting that governments moved slowly. He'd started to feel like he was being left behind, stuck in a dead-end job with a prestigious title that was nothing but a false front. His department budget was slashed, his salary frozen. More funding went to the oil companies and less to the people working to ensure that the same natural resource making the country rich wasn't killing it in other areas.

He'd started to think that if the government didn't care about him, if no one could be bothered to thank him for his tireless work, he didn't care about *it*.

So when he was approached by an oil company representative from another country and offered a substantial sum to sell secrets on Amar's plans—how much oil they were extracting, the price per barrel, how it was being transported and who was buying it—he saw the numbers they offered and had thought it might be a good way to make some fast cash. A small windfall that he could put away for retirement, or at least to make life a little more comfortable while he worked his tail off.

They'd made it easy, too. The representatives were diplomats living in Amar, and they moved in the same circles as himself and the extended relatives of Amar's royal family—fancy events that were fun, but ultimately meaningless when it came to prestige. He'd known that Cally and her late husband had attended these types of events frequently, and had encouraged her to continue that connection to the outside world throughout the course of her grieving process. Uncle Zarek had seen an opportunity, a way to move information in a manner that wouldn't be suspect—and one that would make him look like the good guy to his heartbroken niece.

It was simple. He'd gifted Cally a locket fitted with near-field communication technology inside. With a simple tap of his cell phone, he was able to transfer sensitive information into the locket, which his buyers could then retrieve doing the same thing—a friendly, innocent hug of greeting to Cally, cell phone in hand, meant the transfer was instant and untraceable. Zarek made money, and Cally never had to know about it.

Until she took off to another continent without warning.

Zarek's buyers had been very upset. They'd threatened Cally's life, theorizing she'd figured out the scam and wanted a cut of the money, but Zarek had promised that wasn't the case. He'd told her location to his buyers so they could attempt to retrieve the information, but they grew increasingly violent when she unknowingly foiled them at every turn. The NFC transfer kept getting blocked by her heavy coats and sweaters. When she'd told her uncle about the severity of the attacks during their phone call, he'd realized what was happening and decided he needed to come and retrieve the necklace himself before the buyers took her out—but he couldn't tell the police what he was doing without incriminating himself for treason.

The impatience of her uncle's associates had nearly cost Cally her life. He'd begged for them to be careful, not to use weapons, but when buyers were paying over a million dollars for information that would make them billions, apparently their motto was "by any means necessary."

Cally had left the hospital room in shock. She didn't know if she could ever forgive her uncle, but she supposed it would come in time. She'd returned to the hospital room every day since, trying to make sense of everything.

Even more frustrating was the fact that Aaron's and her paths had crossed very little since that day. She'd been moved to Ellen's apartment to stay with her friend while the official investigation went down and charges were laid, and Cally had been called on several times to make statements. She'd seen Aaron last night at the rehearsal dinner for Ellen's wedding, but there'd been no time to sit and talk about what happened that night—the confession, the kiss.

She sighed, reached over to squeeze her uncle's hand while he slept, then stood with the intention to leave and head down to the wedding reception early.

"Would you like an escort?"

Cally gasped and looked up to see Aaron standing in the doorway. He looked handsome and sleek in his tux, though his expression was uncertain and a mite sheepish.

"Shouldn't you be helping your brother at the photo session?"

He shrugged. "Nah, they're almost done. Sam is finishing up with him. It was my job to bring over any gifts left at the church after the ceremony to the reception venue. I dropped them off and figured...I had a few minutes, and I might find you here. Sorry for startling you. I should have known better—you looked deep in thought. Are you all right?"

"Still asking me that, I see." She offered a gentle smile to ease the sudden worry that flashed across his features. "I appreciate it, Aaron. And I think so. Mostly." She wanted to run over and hug him, but resisted the urge by crossing her arms and hugging her elbows instead. They'd barely connected all week, and she feared that reaching out for an embrace might be unwelcome. "I'm just... I think I'm still in shock. Here I was wondering if maybe I'd done the wrong thing by trying to escape my family, like I was overreacting about their behavior, and then *this* happened. I keep asking God why—why did I feel so strongly that I needed to leave? Was that Him protecting me after all?"

Her words trailed off as she wrenched her gaze from him, feeling foolish, but Aaron moved closer and gripped her forearms. "I can't answer that for you. But I do know that God is good. It sounds like you're still afraid that God was punishing you for running from a hurtful family situation, but from where I stand, it looks like He was actually guiding you to a safer place."

She sighed. "You might be right. If this had happened back home...I feel like the mess would be even worse. Maybe not for my uncle, but for the family in general. At least they can enjoy Christmas without being tied up in the drama. They won't have to deal with it until afterward, when I fly back and tell them the whole story."

"So...you're going back, then?"

Her gaze snapped up. His eyes were wide and sad, like a puppy who'd been scolded. "I do need to talk to them. But believe me, I've considered what it'd be like to just stay here." Her statement was accompanied by a nervous laugh, but she meant it. She'd thought about it a lot, in fact.

"I'd be okay with that."

"You would?"

He shrugged and gestured toward the doors. They walked down the hallway, heading toward the hospital exit. "I meant what I said, Cally. None of that has changed."

"None of what?"

He stopped walking and turned to face her. She'd never seen him so serious. "My feelings for you. You're strong, sensitive and loyal. You know your mind and you refuse to compromise, and I'd never ask you to. Your past makes you who you are today. I want to be a part of your future, if you're willing to make room in your heart for me. I'm madly in love with you, Cally Roslin. And I wouldn't mind if you chose to stay here."

She narrowed her eyes at him, unsure what to make of his admission. Happiness and confusion bubbled up inside of her, mixed with a fear of what might happen the moment she said the words he was waiting to hear, too. She swallowed them down and gave voice to her worry first. "But you might be leaving. For a promotion."

"Well, yes." He tilted his head back and forth. "You could come with me. If you wanted to."

"Aaron."

"I'm serious."

They stepped out the front door onto the sidewalk. The reception was being held in a restaurant banquet room just around the corner. In the time Cally had been visiting her uncle, the sun had set. The sky was dark and clear. Like her thoughts in this moment.

She offered up another reserved, teasing smile. "So, what are you saying?"

He spun around on the sidewalk and dropped to one knee—and then gasped and pointed behind her. She twisted to look over her shoulder and understood his reaction: the northern lights gleamed in the sky overhead, bright shades of green amid the blue-gray night sky.

The sight took her breath away, but it did more than that.

It felt like God's very own love letter to her in this moment, a reminder that He had been with her this whole time. That it was indeed time for a fresh start—a bright renewal of life and love, with someone who understood where she'd come from and what she'd lost, and respected how that fit into who she was and always would be.

Aaron's breath felt warm on her neck. He'd abandoned the whole down-on-one-knee thing and now stood next to her, closer than she could have imagined allowing anyone on that very first day she'd stepped off the little charter airplane.

"Cally?"

Words hung unsaid in the air between them, and she grinned for the first time in a long time, waiting for Aaron to speak them aloud, for the words to reach her. "Yes?"

This time he did slide back down to one knee, the northern lights a stunning backdrop to the moment. "I'm fighting a losing battle here, and to be frank, I don't even want to win. You're the most brave, determined woman I've ever met, and—while it scares me to say this out loud—I'm willing to find a way to make this work if you are. Will you marry me?"

Her heart leaped, telling her—unequivocally—that this was the right time. She had a freelance contract job; she could work from anywhere. Even if he had to move across Canada for a promotion, she'd be willing to follow. It was a startling, but not unwelcome, realization. "You know what? You're the most considerate, attentive, kindest man I know. And handsome, too. I do believe I've fallen in love with you, too...so yes, Officer Thrace. I will marry you."

And when he pulled a thin, silver diamond ring from his pocket and slid it onto her finger, she knew that, despite all that had happened, she was going to have a joyful Christmas after all—making new memories, treasuring the old and looking forward to a grace-filled future.

EPILOGUE

Five and a half years later...

Aaron checked all the buttons and buckles on his ceremonial red RCMP uniform, making sure everything was in place. His brown hat was the final touch, but he wasn't quite ready to put it on yet. He slid his fingers over the brim, stomach twisting with anticipation.

"Ready?" He glanced at Cally, who smoothed her dress and patted her hair before checking her lipstick in a small compact mirror. "You look beautiful. I mean, you always do, but you have an extra sparkle today."

She raised an eyebrow at him. "I'm not sure if I should take that as a compliment…"

He leaned over to kiss her, but she stopped him with a raised hand. "After the ceremony! I didn't bring extra makeup wipes to take red lipstick off your face."

"Good call. And I'll hold you to it. Are all your documents ready?"

Cally lifted a beige envelope from her purse. "If they weren't, it'd be too late to go back and get them." She took a deep breath and exhaled slowly. "We'd better go inside. It's almost time, and we both need to check into our respective places."

He reached for her hand, twining their fingers together. They fit perfectly, as they always had—and today would ensure that they'd stay that way for the rest of their lives, but in a different way than most couples needed to.

Today, Cally would become a Canadian citizen, and he couldn't feel more honored by her choice.

They separated at the front doors as she ventured off to the registration table, where she got in line to check in with her citizenship ceremony notice and other documents. As for him, he'd been appointed as a special guest for this particular citizenship ceremony. It was a gracious gesture by his Ottawa detachment, since they'd known his wife would be taking the oath today.

The way his nerves jumped at every movement, he wondered if he was more anxious about the event than she was.

He met the presiding official and the others who'd be conducting the ceremony, and said his hellos to several fellow officers in attendance—then snuck a glance out the door, eager to watch Cally at every step in the process.

She finished at the registration table and headed into the main room where the ceremony would take place, and minutes later it was time for the event to begin.

He followed the presiding official into the room, which was jam-packed with people about to become new Canadian citizens, as well as their family members, friends and members of the media. Cameras flashed and papers rustled, but he only had eyes for one person. He found her easily: she was sitting in the second row, looking as breathtaking as the moment he'd first laid eyes on her.

His heart beat rapidly in his chest as the presiding official made her opening remarks, after which the applicable guests stood and recited the Canadian oath of citizenship. Cally had brought her family Bible with which to take the oath—a surprising but cherished gift from her mother. Mrs. Roslin had begrudgingly accepted his and Cally's marriage after the first few years, and though it had taken several more for her to finally come around to the idea of Cally becoming a Canadian citizen, mother and daughter had reconciled and the family Bible had been given as a peace offering.

Not everyone in Cally's family felt the same way, but with her mother leading the charge to relate to each other with grace, Aaron had no doubt that Cally would soon feel comfortable taking him on a trip to Amar so that he could meet everyone. He truly looked forward to it.

A lump formed in his throat as Cally's name was called to come forward and receive her certificate of citizenship. She shook the official's hand with one of the biggest smiles he'd ever seen, and he didn't miss her tiny wink in his direction as she returned to her seat. Once all the certificates were handed out, it was time for him to speak.

His speech was short and heartfelt, encouraging the new citizens and congratulating them for their efforts. Although he would never fully relate to their struggles or emotional journey in deciding to call a new country their permanent home, he had no doubt that each and every new citizen had wrestled with the choice and done what was right for them. Cally had come to the decision on her own, surprising him six months ago with the news that she was applying. She'd sent in her application the day she became eligible, five years after being a permanent resident in the country.

Their first five years of marriage hadn't been perfect, but what marriage was? He'd gladly marry her all over again, given the chance.

As the national anthem began to play, he felt certain that both of their voices were louder than the rest of the room—he caught her eye midverse, and the smile she gave him sent a new kind of anxiety swimming around his insides. He wanted to hold her and congratulate her, but it would be a few hours yet before they had a moment alone.

With the official ceremony complete, the reception was held in a side room, where the new citizens could take photos with the presiding official and special guests. Aaron enjoyed this part of his job—everyone loved getting their photo taken with a "real Mountie," and he had fun cracking jokes, posing for pictures and answering questions about horses.

As the room began to clear out, he realized it had been some time since he'd seen his wife. He frowned and scanned the room. Had she stepped outside or wandered off with someone else? He didn't have a message on his phone. He waited a little while longer until only a few folks remained, then made his way to the front entrance.

Cally sat on a bench by the front door, eyes closed. Concerned, he made his way over to her and sat down.

"Sweetheart? Are you doing okay?" He took her hand as she opened her eyes, the corner of her mouth tilting upward. "Feeling overwhelmed? The ceremony is a lot to take in."

"It certainly was, but I'm fine, with regards to that. It was a lovely ceremony, and you gave a great pep talk. I heard a lot of people talking about it afterward."

"Really?"

"Well, sort of." She giggled. "Mostly they were saying how much they liked your hat and comparing you to Mountie characters they've seen on TV and in movies, but still. They *were* talking about you!"

He rolled his eyes, feigning annoyance. He was used to that part of the job by now, and it didn't bother him anymore. Really, so long as public perception of the RCMP was positive, he was doing his job right. "I'm so glad to have helped so many people create their new profile photos for social media."

Cally playfully punched his arm, but her cheerful expression fell away as several caterers came out of the reception room carrying mostly empty trays of sandwiches and other finger foods. The scent of egg salad and deli meats wafted over to the bench where they were seated.

Aaron startled in alarm at the color draining from her face. "Cally! You don't look well. Do you need to get to the washroom? Or a hospital? Was there something wrong with the food?"

She covered her mouth and shook her head, but

sprang off the bench and hurried outside. He followed her, dread in the pit of his stomach.

"Sweetheart, what's going on?"

She waved at him as if he didn't need to be concerned, but he wasn't buying it.

"Tell me how I can help," he said. After such a joyful day, it pained him to see her in distress. "Here, I have a ginger chew in my pocket." He retrieved it and held it out to her. To his great surprise, she took one look at it…and began to laugh. He wasn't sure whether to be relieved or even more worried.

"No, no," she said through gasping breaths, "it's not what you're thinking. I'm fine. Better than fine, in fact. I just…I couldn't be around the smell of that food. It was making me nauseated."

"Was it…" He lowered his voice and looked around, making sure none of the caterers were in earshot. "Off? Not good? I can send in a complaint—"

"Aaron, no. Stop. I'm sure it was delicious. The smell just wasn't agreeing with me. I'm sure you've noticed this happening more than once in the past few weeks."

He thought back, scouring his memory. The details were fuzzy, but he thought he recalled her running from the room when he'd made breakfast a few days ago. He'd assumed she'd needed to check her email or change her shirt, something like that.

"You're telling me those times were related to this?" He was so confused. "What's going on?"

Color slowly came back into her cheeks, but instead of her complexion returning to its usual hue, the rosiness deepened as if she was flushed.

"Well, I wasn't sure until this morning. And then with the ceremony and everything, I wasn't sure how to bring it up, and I didn't know if I wanted to until after today, because…"

Her eyes suddenly filled with tears. He gripped her shoulders and pulled her into his arms, cradling her head to his chest. "Cally, I love you so much. You can tell me anything, anytime. After five years, you have to know that will never change. Whatever it is, we'll get through it together. Just the two of us."

She sniffled again, then drew back, staring at him with a seriousness he'd never seen on her face before. "But, Aaron…what if it's not just the two of us?"

The world dropped away, the way it had only once before. His brain tried to process the words, to catch up to what his heart already understood the moment she glanced down at her middle, hands on her belly.

"Cally? Are we…? Are you saying what I think you're saying?"

She nodded and burst into tears—and so did he.

"We're having a baby," she whispered. "You're going to be a father."

He held her tightly, reveling in the moment, until a thought popped into his head—a thought filled with doubt and anxiety. He held her at arm's length to search her eyes.

"Are you all right with this? I know your relationship with your mother hasn't been ideal, and this means you're about to step into the role…" He let the question linger, but she understood. She nodded and smiled, then held up the family Bible from her own mother.

"A few years ago, I wouldn't have been ready. But I am now."

A family reconciled, a relationship healed and an official beginning united under the same banner. *Thank you, Lord.*

With a greater joy than he'd ever known was even possible, Aaron kissed her—nervous and excited, ready for the days to come, together as a team.

* * * * *

If you enjoyed Christmas Under Fire, *look for the other books in the Mountie Brotherhood series:*

Wilderness Pursuit
Accidental Eyewitness

Dear Reader,

Thank you so much for joining Aaron and Cally during the holidays! No matter where you're from or how you celebrate—or who you celebrate with!—I hope that it's a season of peace and joy for you.

Like Cally, you might have a challenging family situation to manage. Or like Aaron, you may come from a loving, close-knit family that helps each other out in a pinch. Perhaps you're experiencing a season of loss, like Cally, and I think it is especially important to acknowledge that Christmas can be a difficult time for those who are grieving. Wherever God has placed you this holiday season—and whomever He has placed you with—I hope you feel His presence and His grace in the busyness and in the quiet moments.

I'm honored that during the bustle of the season, you've chosen to spend time between these pages. Aaron is the final Thrace brother to be married in the Mountie Brotherhood series, so if you missed Sam's and Leo's stories, be sure to check them out, too!

Blessings,
Michelle

Get 4 FREE REWARDS!

We'll send you 2 FREE Books plus <u>2 FREE Mystery Gifts.</u>

TEXAS RANGER SHOWDOWN
Margaret Daley

SECRET PAST
SHAREE STOVER

Love Inspired® Suspense books feature Christian characters facing challenges to their faith... and lives.

FREE
Value Over
$20

YES! Please send me 2 FREE Love Inspired® Suspense novels and my 2 FREE mystery gifts (gifts are worth about $10 retail). After receiving them, if I don't wish to receive any more books, I can return the shipping statement marked "cancel." If I don't cancel, I will receive 4 brand-new novels every month and be billed just $5.24 each for the regular-print edition or $5.74 each for the larger-print edition in the U.S., or $5.74 each for the regular-print edition or $6.24 each for the larger-print edition in Canada. That's a savings of at least 13% off the cover price. It's quite a bargain! Shipping and handling is just 50¢ per book in the U.S. and 75¢ per book in Canada*. I understand that accepting the 2 free books and gifts places me under no obligation to buy anything. I can always return a shipment and cancel at any time. The free books and gifts are mine to keep no matter what I decide.

Choose one: ☐ **Love Inspired® Suspense**
Regular-Print
(153/353 IDN GMY5)

☐ **Love Inspired® Suspense**
Larger-Print
(107/307 IDN GMY5)

Name (please print)

Address _____ Apt. #

City _____ State/Province _____ Zip/Postal Code

Mail to the Reader Service:
IN U.S.A.: P.O. Box 1341, Buffalo, NY 14240-8531
IN CANADA: P.O. Box 603, Fort Erie, Ontario L2A 5X3

Want to try two free books from another series? Call 1-800-873-8635 or visit www.ReaderService.com.

SPECIAL EXCERPT FROM

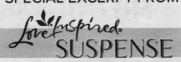

*Robin Hardy may be the only one who can help former
spy Toby Potter—but she can't remember her past with
him or who is trying to kill her.*

*Read on for a sneak preview of
Holiday Amnesia by Lynette Eason,
the next book in the Wrangler's Corner series,
available in December 2018 from
Love Inspired Suspense.*

Toby Potter watched the flames shoot toward the sky as
he raced toward the building. "Robin!"

Sirens screamed closer. Toby had been on his way home
when he'd spotted Robin's car in the parking lot of the lab.
Ever since Robin had discovered his deception—orders
to get close to her and figure out what was going on in
the lab—she'd kept him at arm's length, her narrow-eyed
stare hot enough to singe his eyebrows if he dare try to
get too close.

Tonight, he'd planned to apologize profusely—again—
and ask if there was anything he could do to earn her trust
back. Only to pull into the parking lot, be greeted by the
loud boom and watch flames shoot out of the window near
the front door.

Heart pounding, Toby scanned the front door and rushed
forward only to be forced back by the intense heat. Smoke

LISEXP1118

billowed toward the dark night sky while the fire grew hotter and bigger. Mini explosions followed. Chemicals.

"Robin!"

Toby jumped into his truck and drove around to the back only to find it not much better, although it did seem to be more smoke than flames. Robin was in that building, and he was afraid he'd failed to protect her. Big-time.

Toby parked near the tree line in case more explosions were coming.

At the back door, he grasped the handle and pulled. Locked. Of course. Using both fists, he pounded on the glass-and-metal door. "Robin!"

Another explosion from inside rocked Toby back, but he was able to keep his feet under him. He figured the blast was on the other end of the building—where he knew Robin's station was. If she was anywhere near that station, there was no way she was still alive. "No, please no," he whispered. No one was around to hear him, but maybe God was listening.

Don't miss
Holiday Amnesia *by Lynette Eason,*
available December 2018 wherever
Love Inspired® Suspense books and ebooks are sold.

www.LoveInspired.com

Looking for inspiration in tales
of hope, faith and heartfelt romance?

Check out **Love Inspired**® and
Love Inspired® Suspense books!

New books available every month!

SPECIAL EXCERPT FROM

Love Inspired.

When a young Amish woman has amnesia during the holidays, will a handsome Amish farmer help her regain her memories?

Read on for a sneak preview of
Amish Christmas Memories *by Vannetta Chapman, available December 2018 from Love Inspired.*

"What's your name?"

The woman's eyes widened and her hand shook so that she could barely hold the mug of tea without spilling it. She set it carefully on the coffee table. "I don't—I don't know my name."

"How can you not know your own name?" Caleb asked. "Do you know where you live?"

"Nein."

"What were you doing out there?"

"Out where?"

"Where was your coat and your *kapp*?"

"Caleb, now's not the time to interrogate the poor girl." His *mamm* stood and moved beside her on the couch. She picked up the small book of poetry. "You were carrying this, when Caleb found you. Do you remember it?"

"I don't. This was mine?"

"Found it in the snow," Caleb said. "Right beside where you collapsed."

"So it must be mine."

Caleb noticed that the woman's hands trembled as she opened the cover and stared down at the first page. With one finger, she traced the handwriting there.

LIEXP1118

"Rachel. I think my name is Rachel."

Rachel let her fingers brush over the word again and again. Rachel. Yes, that was her name. She was sure of it. She remembered writing it in the front of the book—she'd used a pen that her *mamm* had given her. She could almost picture herself, somewhere else. She could almost see her mother.

"My *mamm* gave me the pen and the book…for my birthday, I think. I wrote my name—wrote it right here."

"Your *mamm*. So you remember her?"

"Praise be to *Gotte*," Caleb's *dat* said, a smile spreading across his face.

"Is there someone we can call? If you remember the name of your bishop…" Caleb had sat down in the rocker his mother had vacated and was staring at her intensely.

They all were.

She closed her eyes, hoping to feel the memory again. She tried to see the room or the house or the people, but the memory had receded as quickly as it had come, leaving her with a pulsing headache.

She struggled to keep the feelings of panic at bay. Her heart was hammering, and her hands were shaking, and she could barely make sense of the questions they were pelting at her.

Who were these people?

Where was she?

Who was she?

She needed to remember what had happened.

She needed to go home.

Don't miss
Amish Christmas Memories *by Vannetta Chapman,*
available December 2018 wherever
Love Inspired® books and ebooks are sold.

www.LoveInspired.com

Inspirational Romance to Warm Your Heart and Soul

Join our social communities to connect with other readers who share your love!

Sign up for the Love Inspired newsletter at **www.LoveInspired.com** to be the first to find out about upcoming titles, special promotions and exclusive content.

CONNECT WITH US AT:

Facebook.com/groups/HarlequinConnection

 Facebook.com/LoveInspiredBooks

 Twitter.com/LoveInspiredBks